Under
The 13th Star

Selected short fiction, nonfiction, poetry & prose
from The Association of Rhode Island Authors

Under the Thirteenth Star

Selected Short Fiction, Nonfiction, Poetry and Prose
from The Association of Rhode Island Authors

A publication of the Association of Rhode Island Authors
Edited by Lenore M. Rheaume

Table of Contents

Introduction

Under the Thirteenth Star

She was bargained for, as if a key,
Part of the continent, as if brought to light,
Where the natives loved her mightily,
She was bought for pristine brooks, rivers, trees,
But truly it was in this autarchic face, her beauty,
That there was a virtuous place for human will,
And with the hand and mind, almightily,
She was bound for her own illumined glory.

Her little station, cut from plow and shore,
From her tallest trees, ship masts made for sea,
From her vision, in religion, for sacred, free ideals,
For her settlement to harvest prudent farms and fields,
In her spacious harbors, her largess is in civility,
Her flag waves its gentle beginnings, a first democracy,
Furled in white, her golden stars encircle, all thirteen,
With her anchor giving spiritual rest to those who flee.

Today, admired in her little corner of the coast,
She alights the ages, adept of her motto: Hope.

~ Lénore M. Rhéaume

Opening up a new anthology is a marvelous experience, encompassing an amalgamation of creativity, charged by but a few words of commonality. Writers are invited to thread their vision of the chosen theme, to share their individual artistic impression as if designing an intimate quilt. This year, the exposition was to be about the very state they either live in, or describe in their work, or its affectation in their literary essence. Not necessarily describing a location in itself, the writers commingled their niches and

1

ideas about its meaning. So what is there to know about our "Little Rhody?"

Rhode Island's actual official name, the longest moniker of any state in the country, is the "State of Rhode Island and Providence Plantations." It is the tiniest state, about 1200 feet in area, and yet the second most populated as a state in America. Adding to its lengthy name was the merger of four Colonial settlements. Portsmouth and Newport, now referred to as Aquidneck Island, was also called Rhode Island at one time. Roger Williams founded the Providence Plantations which is now the city of Providence and the settlement of Warwick combined. In the last census, there are well over a million residents within the state.

But how is it known to be "thirteen of thirteen?" In May 1776, this "Colony of Rhode Island" was first to separate itself from the Crown of Britain, but by boycotting the 1787 convention that was developing the United States Constitution, it was the last to ratify, in May of 1790. Hence, it became the "thirteenth" state, or last, to sign.

For the Association of Rhode Island Authors, known as ARIA, this became our theme for our second anthology, "Under the Thirteenth Star." The offers of prose and poetry were submitted in numerous genres, uttering many variations as to how their small state inspired their interests in thesis, subject or expression. Nearly two dozen writers from ARIA have come to these pages to contribute pieces of their work. For fiction writers, it may be a portion of a longer work, for others, their non-fiction documents interesting contingents of the area, historical to current. For poets, with New England roots, the environment, the long coastlines, the artistic writ for introspection, all captivate the inventive spirit. The amalgamated beauty of the finished product, resembles a hand sewn quilt, where each individual adds to the pattern their voices, with their unique proclivities assembled in a way which it can form a unanimous whole.

I would like to thank all those that through this collaborative effort brought this work into fruition. It was made with the assistance and dedication of volunteers from ARIA. The process included submission and organization, furthered by a jury of judges and a small staff of editors that chose and read what is included in this volume. Published carefully by those in the association, the final stitching is complete.

Now it is time to sit and enjoy "Under the Thirteenth Star," ARIA's offering to our tiny but mighty Ocean State.

Lénore M. Rhéaume
Poet, Anthology Chair

Short Fiction

The Raid

by L.A. Jacob

L ittle Manny Estrella swung the bucket as he walked up the hill towards St. Patrick's Church. Not quite so little, having inherited his father's broad chest and long legs, at the age of 9, he was the delivery boy for the speakeasy next door to his triple-decker apartment house. Nobody messed with him when he delivered the special medicine that even he knew was liquor from his father's still down in the cellar. The bucket sloshed the liquor around. He could smell its acrid stench as he swung it back and forth, probably dripping some of the precious liquid on the dirt sidewalk.

No one walked this soon after work. Right after work at the Ann & Hope mill, men and women gathered with their families to eat dinner, and then hung out on the stoops if it was too warm. The leaves on the trees in the orchard in the back were already turning, many apples rotting at the base of their trees. However, his father would gather up these bad apples and use them for the still. Old man McAllister didn't seem to mind, as long as his dad didn't pluck them from the tree.

Mrs. Mendoza was busy sweeping out her stoop of non-existent dust. She waved at Little Manny, who waved back. "How's Emma?" she asked in Portuguese.

He replied in the same language, used commonly in the Valley, "Doing better. She got out of bed this morning."

"God bless her," said Mrs. Mendoza, making the sign of the cross. "And your mother."

"Thank you, Mrs. Mendoza," said Manny, echoing the motions. "She should be in church Sunday."

"Come back this way, and I'll give you cookies to give to your mother."

Manny smiled. He'd get a couple of extra for himself, he was sure. "Yes, Mrs. Mendoza."

She smiled and went back into the house. Mrs. Mendoza lived on the first floor of the apartment house, and her husband worked the lathes at the lumberyard outside of the Valley. He wouldn't be home until late.

He went around the corner to the white shingled house with a small front yard and a concrete walkway. He unlocked the gate, and heard a dog bark, a loud, low-pitched bark that held a growl underneath it. Manny knocked on the door and waited.

"Wait! Suave, be quiet!" The door opened and a woman peered out. "Oh, it's you!"

"Hi, Mrs. Alvarez. I'm delivering your special medicine." He held up the bucket.

Mrs. Alvarez was built stocky, like most Portuguese women in the neighborhood. Her husband had lost his arm in an accident in the looms, and her three children worked in the assorted mills near the river. The special medicine was for her husband to sleep at night, she said.

She took the bucket and said, "Wait right there." She stepped back inside, yelling again at the dog, and she came back with a coin. "Here's a quarter for the medicine, and a piece of masa for you."

Mrs. Alvarez handed him the sweet bread, still hot from the oven. "Thank you!" he said, and pocketed the quarter. He was going to get cookies and sweet bread. It couldn't get any better than this.

Upon arriving at Adele's, the speakeasy next to his apartment, his pockets bulged with twisted round cookies for his sisters. He had already eaten the masa, knowing he couldn't stuff it in his pockets.

Adele's didn't even hide itself as an apothecary shop or a drug store, or even any store at all. The blackened windows set high in the building's wall. Without the black paint, they let light into the bar, which lined the entire opposite side of the wall. Adele McAllister

8

manned the bar when he walked in. A few men turned in his direction; he knew them from the neighborhood and greeted them with a wave.

She said in Irish-accented English, "Took you long enough. What's in your pocket?"

Manny took out the quarter and handed it to Adele. "Cookies by Mrs. Mendoza," he replied in English. He knew a lot of English words, and often translated for his father.

Adele took the quarter and put it in her cash box. She turned to one of the men at the bar. "Your neighbor's feedin' the neighborhood kids."

The man shrugged. He didn't speak English, and Adele only knew rudimentary Portuguese, enough to know beer from wine and numbers for money.

"Your father's looking for you," said Adele. "Tell him I need another barrel of that vino."

Manny nodded. He glanced at the trap door to the cellar. He could get to his apartment that way, since that was also the way that the liquor came into the speakeasy. He debated, but the idea was quickly squashed by Adele's glare at him. He put his head down and left through the front door.

He went around the building to the back door of the apartment, which led directly into the kitchen. He could smell dinner wafting through the open window. Stew again, but that was all the family really had. His mother's chourice in the smokehouse out back was still drying and wouldn't be ready for another couple of months.

He threw open the door and saw his mother, Rose, at the kitchen stove, stirring a pot. "Manny," she said, and gave him a quick hug when he approached. "Go sit with Alice and Slugger until dinner's ready. Elsie's there, but you know her."

Alice, his oldest sister, was going out with "Slugger" Santos. They always had to have a chaperone, and Elsie, dreamy, distracted Elsie, was there with them. She would listen to the radio with her ear against the speaker, immersing herself into the world of the radio, no matter what was on. A train could come through the house and she wouldn't even notice, which made her a horrible chaperone.

Manny bounded into the living room, with a loud, "Hello!" as he jumped over the threshold and landed, his arms spread wide like Fred Astaire coming down from a high pirouette. As he expected, Alice and Slugger jumped slightly while sitting on the couch.

Alice was tall for her 15 years. With long, thick, raven hair down to her mid-back, black, deep, soulful eyes, she was slightly disproportionate with broad shoulders and hips, but someone obviously found her attractive. She told him, slightly annoyed, "Don't do that, Manny."

Slugger had broad shoulders too, but he was chiseled out of the rock that came out of the Blackstone Mines. Square face, square jaw, short-cropped black hair, he was nicknamed not for his boxing ability, but his use of a baseball bat during baseball games. He was going to try and become a cop—his father was a guard at the Ann & Hope Mill, and he knew people. The force was full of Irishmen from Lonsdale, while the Valley started to get filled with the Portuguese from the Azores.

Manny dropped on the couch next to his sister. He pulled out one of the now-broken cookies from Mrs. Mendoza. "Want a cookie?" Elsie was on the floor, listening intently to the commercial for Palmolive.

"That'll ruin your dinner," said Alice, eyeing the cookie. She took it anyway. Manny pulled out another piece and waved it in front of Elsie, like a string for a cat to pay with. Elsie grabbed the cookie.

Manny didn't offer one to Slugger. He didn't like Slugger, didn't like the fact that Slugger was holding his sister's hand. Manny looked at the hand-holding intently, as if his eyes would be able to pare them apart. Alice let go and placed her hand on her lap.

Scoring a victory, he tried to stare at Slugger to get him to leave. Alice said to him, "Are you sick or something?"

Manny sat back. "Nope," he said.

Slugger sighed. He said, "You're old enough that we can be alone."

"You should say something, then."

"Me? It's your mother."

"Will your mother let us sit alone or will we have to deal with her being in the same room, too?"

Slugger was now an only child, his brother and sister having died at an early age. Slugger shrugged again.

Alice crossed her arms. "See?"

Slugger looked at Elsie, who didn't even look like she was paying attention. He glanced up at the cuckoo clock. "I should go home anyway. Your father will be home soon."

Alice got up at the same time Slugger did. They went to the door that led out into the small hallway, leading out front. Slugger lived a few trolley stops away in Central Falls. Manny followed to make sure that there wouldn't be any hanky-panky.

There wasn't, not even a chaste kiss on the cheek. A squeeze of hands and Slugger stepped out onto the sidewalk. He took maybe five steps to the trolley stop, and waited. Alice stood at the door, watching.

Manny said disgustedly, "Every night you watch him get on the trolley. He's not going to get hit by a car."

"You don't understand," she said. She waited until he got on the trolley and then went back inside.

"Alice! Set the table. Manny! Go outside in the garden and get some tomatoes."

When Manny came in with the tomatoes, he saw his father's lunch bucket on the chair, and heard him washing up in the bathroom. He dropped his tomatoes on the counter and went to the bathroom.

His father, a big, broad man, had finished his twelve-hour shift at the Lonsdale Bleachery. He loaded and unloaded textiles from the trains, and had just been given the duties of an assistant supervisor with an extra half-penny an hour for the compensation.

His father took a towel from the rack and saw him. Manuel smiled and rustled Little Manny's hair. Without any other words of greeting he went out of the bathroom to the kitchen.

Little Manny's mother was spooning out the stew when Manuel entered. He sighed, sat down at the head table. Little Manny went to get Elsie.

Elsie was sitting with her ear against the speaker. "Dinner," he called. She looked up, her deep brown eyes glassy with being in another world. He reached over and shut off the radio.

She blinked for a minute, coming back to the present. "Dinner?" she said.

Manny held a hand down for her to help her stand. She stood, wobbling a little. She went into the kitchen.

There was only enough room for four, which was fine, because his mother never sat down to eat until after everyone else had eaten. His father grunted like a pig as he ate, stuffing stew into his maw while his mother kept telling Little Manny to keep his elbows off the table. Manuel held up his bowl for seconds, and Rose rushed to get it. She was not stocky like the other Portuguese women, but thin and with an hourglass shape that Alice emulated. Alice, Manny knew, used a corset; he wondered if his mother did, too.

Manuel finished, sitting back, and looking over his brood of children, eating slowly and daintily, not slurping from the bowl, not sticking bread in the stew, but sipping from the spoon. "You gotta have manners in this world," he started to lecture the kids. "My papa, my vovo, we never had any manners growing up. We milked the cows and came right in to eat without washing up." He picked at his teeth with the knife. He looked to Manny. "I think it's time you start working like your sisters."

Manny looked to his mother. She was washing dishes that had suddenly appeared in the sink. "Papa," said Manny, "I have a job."

"Delivering liquor to people too lazy to make it to the bar?" Manuel said. "How much do you make?"

"Mrs. Mendoza gave me a cookie. And Mrs. Alvarez gave me some masa."

Manuel snorted. "Did you bring any of it home?"

"I got a cookie," said Elsie.

Manuel said, "I didn't get a cookie."

Alice snickered, but at a look from her father, she shut up. Manuel said to Manny, "We're going over there tonight and tell Mrs. Adele to pay you from now on. A penny a delivery. That seems fair."

"Yes, papa," said Manny, and passed his bowl to his mother, who promptly washed it.

After dinner, and while Rose went to feed Emma, Manuel and Manny went around the corner to Adele's. A man sat on the stairs of the speakeasy, looking like any other man, smoking and watching the street. He nodded to the father and son as Manuel pushed open the door.

Cigarette smoke assaulted them, making Manny cough. His father smoked, too, but in here, everyone smoked, all the time, so the air hung heavy with burnt tobacco. Adele was manning the bar with her brother Tommy, who caught Manuel's eye when they first entered. He ribbed his sister, who switched sides with Tommy.

"And how's my best supplier?" she asked in English.

Manny translated for his father. "I need to get Manny a job. He needs to start pulling his weight."

"Aren't the mills hiring?"

"I want you to pay Manny a penny a delivery."

"A penny! That's robbery."

Manuel shrugged. "I don't have to give you the good white wine, either." He leaned forward on the bar. "If he gets enough pennies, he can get a bike, and deliver farther. Maybe to Lonsdale or Central Falls."

"I'll get him a bike," said Tommy.

Adele looked like she was chewing on the idea. "Let me think about it."

Manuel said to Manny, "No deliveries until she pays you." Then he said to Adele, "Uma carveja."

She racked up one beer. "Don't want your own rotgut?"

"Why should I buy my own booze?" Manny translated Adele's words without "rotgut." She laughed, went back to her place at the other end of the bar.

They stayed for a short time, long enough to get the smoke smell saturated in their clothes. Mama Rose laid into both of them, saying that now she had to wash these clothes because they would stink up the apartment and the hamper.

Emma was sitting up in bed when Manny kissed her good night. All the kids lined up in her room and Alice and Elsie climbed into bed with her. Manny got to sleep at the foot of the bed, because he was getting older now and couldn't sleep with his sisters anymore. They didn't have enough money to get another bed, and they didn't have the room in the tiny two-bedroom apartment to put another bed.

The next morning, Manny helped his mother get together the lunches for the girls and his father. The girls would go work at the lace factory near the river, while his father worked a few doors down at the Bleachery. Emma was still asleep in bed. Said Manuel, "Your mother and I talked last night, Manny. I'm going to find you a job in the Bleachery or somewhere else in the mills."

"No more deliveries?"

"Along with the deliveries. There's nothing wrong with two jobs."

Manny looked down. "Yes, Papa."

Manuel said sternly, "It's time you start acting like a man of this house."

"Yes, Papa."

After his father left, and Manny watched his father and sisters walk south toward the mills, Manny scampered outside to Adele's. She was open, even at this early hour, and had three buckets lined up on the counter. "A half-penny a delivery," she said. "How does that sound?"

He would be rich in no time. He nodded. She shoved two of the buckets toward him. "Two go to Mr. Chace near the orchard. Go in the back door, you know the rules."

"Yes, Mrs. Adele."

"The last one goes to Queen Mary."

Manny snickered. They called her Queen Mary because she was an Irish snob in the neighborhood. She "knew people."

"Come back for noon and I'll have more."

He made his deliveries, and it wasn't until the afternoon when saw the policemen on Broad Street. They drove slowly down the street, one of the cops with his head hanging out, almost smelling the air for something. He didn't wear a uniform, but looked like he wore a suit. Manny ducked into a store while the car went by. A woman screamed, and he saw it was a beauty parlor.

He jumped out quickly and ran up the street, holding the bucket close to him so that it wouldn't slosh all over the place. He turned a corner onto Maple Street and found his way to the house he was meant to deliver it to. He ran back to Adele's, careful to watch for that cop car.

"Mrs. Adele," he said, out of breath, and he put his hands on his thighs, bent over to try and catch his breath.

Adele waited. "Coppers," he finally said.

Adele smiled. "I pay my way. They don't bother me."

He shook his head. "Don't know this copper. He smells booze."

Adele's smile turned to a frown. "Where's the money?"

He took out the quarters, and Adele gave him his penny. Then she went to the phone. "Ellie? Can you ring Leon?" She hummed to herself as the call went through. "Leon. I heard something about—they are?" She turned to look at Manny, her eyes now wide. She let out a few words in Irish that Manny didn't understand, and the conversation took place in that language. She slammed down the phone and leaned on the bar. To the two patrons there, she said,

"Get out! Manny, go downstairs and—and," she didn't know what else to say. She was shaking.

"Mrs. Adele?" Manny went behind the bar.

"My God, the feds are in town. They're gonna raid us. You have to tell your papa. I got eight barrels downstairs!"

Said one of the men at the bar, "Call Danny."

Adele whirled on the man. "Danny. Danny Walsh? What pound o' flesh will he take outta me if I do?"

"Either him or the feds," said the man, draining his beer quickly and heading out the door.

Manny was alone with Adele, who paced back and forth along the wooden boards behind the bar, wearing out another patch. "Omygod, what do I do?"

"Who's Danny?"

"A mover," she said shortly. "Go run home and tell your Ma. They're gonna raid you too if they see the dumbwaiter. Go, go!"

Manny ran out of the bar and into his house. His mother was washing clothes on the wooden washboard in the tub. "Mama, the feds are here."

His mother dropped everything into the tub. "Where?"

"They're going to raid Mrs. Adele and maybe us too."

"Come downstairs." She got up and they went down into the cellar. He could see the still against the wall, the one that made the moonshine from the rotting apples in the orchard, and the vats full of fermenting grape juice for the red wine. A few empty barrels stood on one side of the dumbwaiter, that only went up about three feet to Adele's cellar, and then would roll out onto her dirt-packed floor. It was easier to build that than a ramp.

He and his mother moved the barrels next to the still. Then they got a wooden screen and placed that against the still. The vat they couldn't help; they drained it into barrels and rolled the barrels up the stairs. They placed the barrels out back and poured the grape juice into the garden.

They were still working when the girls got home, and they were enlisted to help. At the same time, Manny saw a fleet of cars and trucks near Adele's. As Manny was rolling one of the barrels to the back door, he saw a man come toward him. Built solid, he wore a t-shirt with a pack of cigarettes rolled in one sleeve and home-sewn dungarees. He looked like a dockworker, with his splash of red hair. He smiled at Manny. "Need help w' tha'?"

Manny had been doing it all day, and he could use a rest. He nodded. The man whistled. Two other big men came over, one effortlessly lifting the barrel onto his shoulder. The second man and the one with the cigarettes went to his mother in the garden.

They spoke in low tones, as his mother brought the man down into the cellar. They brought up more barrels, but this time took the barrels to their trucks. Now things were moving faster.

Manny stayed out of the way. The men finished just before his father got home, who immediately started screaming at his mother. The kids scattered, running into the house. Manny followed, and sat cowering at the foot of Emma's bed, Elsie and Alice in the bed with Emma.

"Manuel!" yelled his father from the kitchen. Manny knew he was in trouble when his father used his full name like that. He blinked away tears, tears that would probably send his father into a rage, and he stood up at the foot of Emma's bed. The three girls, their eyes wide, stared at him as he straightened his shirt and gulped.

"Manuel!" yelled his father again, and Manny heard him trooping to Emma's doorway. He stepped out from behind the foot of the bed and met his father at the threshold.

His father grabbed him by the ear and yanked him out into the kitchen. His mother sat quietly, her hands on her lap, her head down. He thought he could see a bruise forming on her face.

"Tell me the truth," said his father, just as there was a knock on the outside front door.

His father glanced in the direction of the doorway. He seemed undecided for a moment. The knock came again, much louder this time. Manuel tossed Manny so hard he fell against the wall and onto his butt. Manuel went to answer the door.

Manny heard his father yell for him again. He got up off the floor as his mother stood up, straightening her apron. Manny ran to the front door to see the man in a suit from this afternoon and three policemen at the door. "What are they saying?" his father asked him.

"They want to come in to look around."

"Tell them no."

But one of the cops must have understood what his father said, and he shoved by his father to come into the hallway. The hallway led to the apartment, and the three cops stormed into the place. His father was beside himself, yelling at them in Portuguese, while Manny tried to move out of the way of the men. They went into Emma's room, looking in the wardrobe and under the bed.

Then they went into the cellar.

His father followed them. The man in the suit led the way, and immediately bee-lined for the vat. "What's in here?" It was the first time he spoke. He had a touch of an accent, southern perhaps.

Manny translated for his father. "We make wine. We cook with it."

"This is a very big vat," said the man. "You must cook with it a lot."

His father motioned outside. "We use it for chourice, outside, in the smokehouse."

"Do you sell them to anyone?"

"No, of course not."

The man in the suit didn't look like he believed it. Manny noticed one of the cops standing near the false wall that hid both the dumbwaiter and the still. Manny looked at the cop, who gave him a wink.

"Nothin' down here," said one of the cops to the man in the suit.

He looked disgusted, got in close to his father. "You watch your step, Portagee."

His father said, "Eu nao entendo." He didn't understand. But Manny knew he did, just by the angry look on his face.

The man in the suit huffed at him, pulled out a cigarette and started up the stairs. He lit it at the top of the stairs. "Let's go," he said to the cops, and they all filed out the front door.

The family breathed when the man and the cops left. His father said to his mother, "Where's dinner?"

His mother jumped to scrape together some spicy egg sandwiches.

His father never apologized, but, then it wasn't expected. The next morning Manny went to Adele's but the door was locked. The day after that his father brought him to the mill to present him to his foreman. Judged "too scrawny" for the Bleachery, he was dragged away to the looms to work there for the day, and for the next ten years until the mill closed.

On Sunday, his mother got Emma up to go to church. Everyone in the family went to church that Sunday, up the road to St. Patrick's. Manny saw Adele there, and told her that he was working in the looms now, and couldn't be her delivery boy.

She smiled at him, patted him on the head, and told him, "I couldn't afford ya, anyway."

The Confession of Esek Kenyon

by Steven R. Porter

It is for the sake of God's grace, and for the pitiful defense of my own frayed soul, that I must now record the details of this grotesque and disturbing matter to the permanence of ink and paper. In my earliest years, I vowed to live my life as a man of honor and conscience, and except for this one brooding, regrettable incident, I swear that I have paid resolute allegiance to that sacred pledge. But the jaws of guilt gnaw incessantly at the lining of my stomach, and I admit that I can no longer bear the wretched pain. And now as I lay here rotting in a festering pool of my own fetid sweat, alone in this world except for the companionship of a compassionate nurse, I have accepted that my eternity truly lies with the devil; and I know that as I write, he is gleefully preparing for our inevitable meeting at the inhospitable wrought-iron gates of hell. I pray that with this declaration of truth, heaven may shower but a sliver of its pity upon me.

I was a mere twenty-two years of age when Gorton and I, employed as caretakers of the old Congdon Estate, noticed the wretched boys stumbling like drunkards in the darkness along the deer path at the base of Nooseneck Hill. There were three of the poor, wretched souls, aged no more than sixteen years, each one more filthy, gangly and misshapen than the other. One appeared to be missing an eye, another a hand and the third walked along on a twisted, grotesque stump that had once been a right foot. The trio was illuminated by a waning moon that shone just past full, and behind them, despite the hour, we could see plainly that the boys were dragging a white marble headstone.

Gorton spied the boys first, and they startled as he shined the beam of his searchlight into all five of their good eyes. These humbly-bred country boys snarled like feral cats and recoiled, one of them releasing a ghastly shriek that wrinkled my skin and stiffened my spine. We already knew they were returning from the notorious Congdon burial plot. Odd sightings and disturbing moans that rose from the gaseous, murky swamps that surrounded the graves were well-rumored in these parts, attracting roguish youths, adventurous trespassers and devout ritualists all looking either for a shameful thrill at the expense of the Congdon family's poor, departed ancestors or for an unnatural connection between this life and the next.

My colleague, Mr. Gorton, who by day tended Providence's esteemed Swan Point Cemetery, was an experienced, even-tempered man who championed fact and logic, never conceding his good sense to the creatures others suppose crouched in the shadows, never fearing tales of serpents that lurk beneath the waves preparing to nourish themselves on the tender flesh of dim-witted sailors, and never flinching at thoughts of the soft, warm-bodied, fleshy things that scurry at night inside cabin walls. Even with my youthful instincts, I sensed these boys reeked of death. I could feel the unnatural doom lapping at us on the tongue of the wind. Yet I refused to concede my self-control to any irrational creeping fear. I took strength from Gorton, and from my duty, and merely writhed my hands, struggling to keep the facts from transforming into insane delusion.

The taller of the boys spoke and spit through broken teeth, slurring a creepy, mumbled apology. Gorton waved an authoritative bony fist and shouted at them to be gone, causing the three to scamper like mischievous sprites into the underbrush and disappear from our sight. He tossed the end of the boys' rope at me and ordered me to pull. We must return the stone to the grave of the poor wretched soul who had lost it. I crouched to read the inscription:

Prudence Congdon
B. 16 June 1904
D.

As we dragged the stone back up Nooseneck Hill, I pondered the subject of the demise of the unfortunate Miss Prudence. Her memorial stone bore no date of death, no spouse, no other family member nor any obvious religious affiliation. Might she still be alive? Or might she have been the last of her strain, exhaling her final breath friendless, enduring a lonely death with no relations left to honor her life and inscribe even her most humble date of passing? It also struck me as peculiar that the stone was clean, appearing to shine and emote an unnatural glow in the moonlight. All those schizophrenic New England springs, summers, autumns and winters had left no noticeable trace of filth, grime or wear upon it, and it was as if the stone had toppled off the stonecutter's bench that very moment, or perhaps it had been painstakingly polished at the hand of a resolute agent.

But no man could have prepared us for the ghastly scene Gorton and I would encounter at the gates of that small family graveyard. We stood aghast, hypnotized with horror. I could feel the devil's own arm wrap itself gently around my shoulders, as if welcoming me at his door, a surprise guest at some grisly social occasion. Ahead of us, three graves laid open and freshly exhumed. I choked in nausea at the stench of ancient, rotted flesh and dank soil that hung heavy in the moist air. Shards of coffin parts littered the ground while the burial cloths and garments of the dead, now only unrecognizable bits of stained, frilly rags, hung among the shrubbery fluttering like gruesome flags in the foul autumn breeze.

Oh, what thoughts I had! To this day, I regret not conceding to my first instinct, which was to turn and run from this ghoulish nightmare and purge from my memory any recollection of this terrible scene. But before I had the chance to submit to my senses and flee, Gorton grabbed my forearm and pulled me towards him. His fingernails pierced my flesh. He had barely uttered a sound since we had started up the hill, and he said but one sentence now.

"Esek, we've made a terrible mistake."

Gorton bolted into the graveyard frantically collecting debris and tossing it back into the holes, his eyes exploding from his forehead as he scrambled. He shouted, cursed and begged for my help.

Since I was loyal to the man, I was able to find a reserve of energy and denial from somewhere deep within my bowels, and I joined him.

We worked feverishly through the night moving earth and debris, and at the setting of the moon, we were forced to endure our labor in near total blackness. My head ached from the stress of terror that would have driven a better man to madness, my parched throat nearly swelled closed in fright. When the sun did rise many hours later, we were exhausted, but the holes were filled. And with a few armfuls of well-scattered leaves collected from the nearby knotty oaks and red maples, we left the impression nothing had ever happened. I was so ragged from our gory ordeal I never bothered to read the headstones of those three open graves: *George Congdon, Philip Congdon,* and *Raymond Congdon.* My nurse would later explain that the brothers— all teens— had died of influenza in that horrific winter of 1918.

And so, it was. To all who read this, that is my confession. Despite the depth of my despair and misery, I feel curiously nostalgic as I ponder those foolish, unenlightened days of my youth when my soul was stainless and my body immortal.

Yet the great irony is this. As I impatiently wait for my own moment of death or for that last moment of clarity before I slip into eternal psychotic madness, I pray that my dutiful nurse, Prudence, will read this heartfelt confession and accept it as an appeal for her forgiveness. I do understand why her brothers had been so eager to honor her passing that night so many years ago. Prudence had been brutally murdered, her body snatched up by a cowardly assailant and buried without ceremony beneath the great sand banks on the other side of town. Brokenhearted, the boys dug their way up from the depth of their own graves to deliver that stone in her honor. And by filling in those three holes, Old Gorton and I inadvertently sealed the boys' eternal fate as well, relegating their spirits to forever limp in the shadows with their beloved sister, to never again enjoy the comfort of perpetual rest.

C.Y.A.

by Tom Trabulsi

"Jesus, Mikey, where's all that blood coming from?"

As the officer in charge of Rescue 2, Lieutenant Mike Doneen owned this whole scene. His partner, a private named Jimmy Rodell, had already climbed into the backseat of the car. Lt. Doneen could not believe how much blood there was. "Row, man, watch out. It's fucking everywhere."

Rodell should have cared but there was no time. The car was embedded head-on into a tree. The unrestrained driver was strewn across the frontseat with both feet somehow jammed beneath the brake pedal. Rodell climbed over the seat, posted his left hand on the cushion, and reached with his right to free the driver's feet. The struggle drove his left hand deeper until the pooling blood flooded his glove. "Where the fuck are the engine guys?"

"I got his neck done." Lt. Doneen had the guy collared in case of fracture. The driver gasped, gurgling blood with wide open eyes that saw nothing. Lt. Doneen could already tell by the unequal pupils that a severe head injury had likely torn through his brain. He turned to the half-dozen cops that wanted nothing to do with this mess. "Was he talking when you guys got here?"

"Never said a word," one of them answered.

Engine 2 finally screeched to a stop. Three firemen grabbed a stretcher and backboard from the rescue and headed for the car.

"Sorry we're late," Captain Sousa said. "Got jammed up behind school buses. What do you need?"

"Load and go, Cap." Lt. Doneen felt for a pulse on the guy's neck. "He's lost so much blood he might code at any second."

They shoved the backboard beneath the driver, strapped him down, and dragged him onto the stretcher.

25

"Let's go!"

When Rodell pulled off his flooded glove, the blood splashed across the street in a macabre design. Inside the rescue, Lt. Doneen suctioned more blood and broken teeth out of the airway. "Let's cut off his clothes and find out where all this blood is coming from. Then let's start two large bore IV's for fluid."

They used trauma shears to cut through the blood-soaked clothes. In unison, they rolled him onto his side to inspect his back. Rodell looked at his boss. "There ain't nothing here, man. Internal hemorrhage?"

"Yeah, he must've ruptured something." Lt. Doneen looked at Capt. Sousa. "I need two of your guys."

"Roger that. Phipps, you drive them. Lenny, help these guys back here. I'll follow in the truck."

Rodell and Lenny had already started an IV in either arm with two bags of fluid running wide open. This was against protocol with a suspected brain injury, but that wouldn't matter if the guy died from blood loss.

Lt. Doneen pumped a bag-valve mask over the guy's mouth and nose. "Let's get him on the monitor and see what his heart's doing."

Rodell attached the EKG pads as the three of them watched the monitor. "Shit, dude, I think we're losing him."

Lt. Doneen yelled, "Phipps! Let's get going!"

The heart rate went from 40 beats per minute, to 30, 20, flatline.

"Fuck me." Lt. Doneen kept bagging him. "Row, CPR. Lenny, get the Epi. Phipps, let's go, dude!"

"Roger!" Once the rescue lurched forward, the three of them tried to maintain their balance like fishermen on a storm-tossed boat.

Lt. Doneen bagged him while toggling his microphone. "Rescue 2 to Fire Alarm."

Dispatch answered, *"Fire Alarm's on, Rescue 2."*

"Advise Rhode Island Hospital we have a twenty-something male unrestrained driver who struck a tree. He has cuts and deformities to the left side of his face but no other visible injuries. This is now a trauma code. Two IV's established, two rounds of epinephrine on board, CPR's in progress. We're ten minutes out."

"Roger that, Rescue 2."

Lt. Doneen directed the code as they transported. On shift for barely an hour, he knew this was a bad omen for the career-ending judgment that may or may not arrive at 3:00 PM today. But he couldn't think about that now. "Yo, Row? What's our saying?"

"You can die at your house or the hospital, but you can't die here."

"Hell yeah, son."

As the ambulance tore a seam through the rush hour traffic, those on their way to work remained oblivious to the mortal struggle contained therein.

***

An hour later, after the truck was decontaminated and restocked, they left the hospital. The morning commute was a brick wall, so I-95 was going nowhere.

When Lt. Doneen felt Rodell turn and look at him, he immediately said, "No."

"Aw, come on, man, we started the day with two shitty runs and haven't even had time for coffee."

"Please, dude. Last time we went lights and sirens for no reason we almost got into a wreck. They would've busted our ass for that."

The radio suddenly said, *"Fire Alarm to Rescue 2."*

Lt. Doneen grabbed the microphone. "Rescue 2."

"Status?"

"Just cleared RIH but not yet in the city. You gotta run for us?"

"*Affirmative. Start responding with Engine 3 to the boat ramp at Tim Healy Way for a reported ETOH with injuries.*"

"Bring it on." Rodell hit the lights and sirens. "The rescue gods must be out to get us."

The city of Pawtucket appeared around the bend. Once the epicenter of the Industrial Revolution, this still proud city had been on a decades long decline. With most of its fifty mills now empty and shuttered, the jobs and middle class were being hunted into extinction. Left behind were the elderly in homes they'd owned for sixty years, and a working class filled with immigrants just trying to get ahead.

"Engine 3 to Rescue 2."

Lt. Doneen said, "Rescue 2."

"Lou"—Captain Conlin used the slang for lieutenant—"gotta frequent flyer here. Vitals stable. Use caution responding."

"Roger that."

Behind the wheel, Rodell grinned and said, "It's probably Eddy."

"I hope not. Yesterday he was covered in puke."

The homeless had taken to gathering in certain spots around the city, but Asshole Tree is where the die-hard drunks schemed and fought. Rescue 2 peeled off the highway and circled back beneath the bridge. Behind Engine 3, Captain Conlin awaited. He said, "Well, if it isn't the Brothers Grimm."

Since both had shaved heads and matching attitudes, their nickname was now part of the department vernacular. It was a unique pairing. Lieutenant Doneen was twenty-nine, had been on the fire department for eight years, and was widely considered a rising star. Rodell, an avid tri-athlete, was twelve years older, but, having worked construction for two decades, was in better shape than most of the twenty-year-olds in his academy class.

Lt. Doneen asked Capt. Conlin, "So who we got?"

"Fitz."

"Gross." Rodell snapped gloves on and grabbed the trauma bag. "He piss himself again?"

28

"Yup. And someone beat his ass."

Fitz was seated on the front bumper of the engine. After his wife died, Fitz, a former city worker, had decided to drink himself to death. Worse, he lived in the streets even though he owned a home he refused to live in without her.

Lt. Doneen said, "Jesus, Fitzy, this ain't no way to spend your retirement."

Surrounded by cops and firemen, Fitz was growing agitated. "Them kids busted my nose."

"We picked you up twice yesterday." Rodell dabbed the blood off Fitz's face. "And here it is, not even 9:30."

Lt. Doneen said, "What do you say, Fitz? You want to go to the hospital?"

"No thank you." But then he promptly face-planted off the bumper.

"Seriously?" Rodell helped him up. "You're coming with us or we're just gonna get called right back after someone sees you passed out on the sidewalk. Again."

"My partner's right. Besides, you can't hardly stand."

"Aw, come on, guys."

"Fitz, you know the deal. Hospital or the cops take you to jail. Your choice."

"Aw ..." He batted a hand. "At least I'll get clean clothes and food at the hospital."

"I'm sure the taxpayers appreciate that. Hell, this'll make three visits to the ER inside twenty-four hours. Might be a new record."

"Negative," Rodell said. "Slime-Pants pulled down a four-spot last summer, remember?"

Captain Conlin graveled a cigarette burnt chuckle. "You boys are off to some start."

"Going out with a bang." Lt. Doneen was only half-kidding. "Today's the day, right?"

"Three o'clock. Honestly, I just want this over with."

"Me too," Rodell added, walking Fitz to the truck. "It's like coming to work everyday with a knife at our throats."

Captain Conlin said, "Union lawyer say anything?"

"Fifty-fifty. Ain't that some shit?"

"Damn."

"Yeah, after everyone else's fuck-ups buried the guy before we even got on-scene."

Rodell opened the back of the rescue and said, "Thought we said we weren't gonna talk about it?"

"You're right." Lt. Doneen turned to Conlin. "We're all set, Cap. You guys can clear."

"See you at the next one."

Because of the urine, they put Fitz on the benchseat. As they took vitals and a blood sugar, a call went out for a diabetic emergency two blocks away. Lt. Doneen knew protocol only allowed one patient per rescue, but after he heard the description of a green Chevrolet, it sounded like another frequent flyer.

Rodell was reading his mind. "Might be Gary."

"Could be." Lt. Doneen toggled the shoulder-mic on his portable. "Rescue 2 to Fire Alarm."

"Go ahead, Rescue 2."

"We're gonna take that. We're right around the corner. Did an elderly female call 911?"

"Roger. She's in the car and says her son passed out."

"Keep Engine 3 on this for man-power just in case."

"Roger. Fire Alarm to Engine 3?"

Captain Conlin said, "Engine 3 receive's that. En route."

Rodell took two right turns and found the green Chevrolet resting against a telephone pole. "Check this out. Least he didn't crash it."

Lt. Doneen poked his head through the hatch connecting the patient compartment to the cab. "Wow, look at that."

Rodell grabbed the microphone. "Rescue 2's on scene."

"Rescue 2's on scene at 0926."

Lt. Doneen hopped out with the diabetic bag, which contained Glucagon, syringes, different gels and goos for conscious patients, and for the unconscious an IV set-up for a D-10 dextrose drip.

They found 375 pound Gary Janowski sound asleep behind the wheel. Head thrown back, he loudly snored. A nice old lady next to him smiled and said, "Good morning, Lieutenant."

"Hello, Mrs. Janowski, what's the occasion? You're all dressed up today."

"Daily vespers." Her wrinkles spread into a wide smile. "Gary was just taking me to Saint Theresa's."

"He check his sugar today?"

"Yes, but he's been fighting to keep it up all morning."

"He eat breakfast?"

"Yes. Eggs and toast."

While Lt. Doneen asked the questions, Rodell had opened the driver's door and drew blood off Gary's fingertip. Seconds later the glucometer read 21 when it should have been 70 or above.

"Uh-oh." Rodell showed it to his boss. "*No bueno.*"

"*Mucho no bueno.*" Lt. Doneen turned to Mrs. Janowski. "We're gonna hit him with an IV."

Engine 3 made the corner and roared to a stop. Captain Conlin saluted Lt. Doneen and said, "Long time no see. What do you need, lou?"

"His sugar's twenty-one. We're gonna whack him with the D-10. Mom says he's been fighting it all morning."

"Where's Fitz?"

"Already passed out. I wasn't about to drag Rescue 1 across the city for this. Besides, he ain't going nowhere."

From experience, Rodell knew Gary had one vein left. Diabetics were always a tough stick, but diabetic former heroin addicts were a thousand times harder. Known as the local boy made good/gone bad, Gary Janowski was once an accomplished cellist for the Boston Symphony. That was before a car wreck strung him out on opiates. Rodell pulled off the sock and held the swollen purple foot. It was a pressure-filled moment, because if Rodell missed and blew their only vein, access for rapid intervention was gone.

Lt. Doneen readied the D-10, which was an IV bag containing dextrose. Rodell advanced the needle into Gary's foot and he didn't even twitch. They connected the IV to the catheter, let it run wide open, and within two minutes the sugar rolled Gary's eyes wide open.

"Hey, Gary."

"Lieutenant Mike." Gary blinked. "Uh-oh."

"Don't move your foot." Rodell braced his calf. "Careful, we got you all dialed in."

"Welcome back, honey." Mrs. Janowski stroked his sweaty chin as only a mother could. "Think maybe you should go to the hospital and get checked out?"

"I'd rather—"

"Gary," Lt. Doneen said, "mom says you've been chasing it all morning. Get checked out. You never know. Later today you might be doing sixty down the highway."

Gary Janowski looked down at his tiny mother. "Can you drive this to Memorial?"

"Of course, dear, it's only a couple of blocks away."

Rodell drew fresh blood and this time the glucometer read 151. "Now that's more like it."

"Okay, Gary," Lt. Doneen said. "Let's go. Careful with the foot."

Inside the truck, Fitz, seatbelted onto the benchseat, broke out a drunken grin. "Welcome aboard, matey. Ha-ha-ha!"

"Easy, Fitz." Rodell said as Lt. Doneen worked the computer. "This ain't no disco."

"Ah-ha-ha-ha-ha!"

On the stretcher, Gary's nostrils flinched. "My new friend here is quite aromatic."

"I like that word." Rodell glanced at his boss. "Aromatic 2, transporting to Memorial."

They pulled into the hospital minutes later. They got Fitz a wheelchair and brought Gary in by stretcher. Inside, the charge nurse shot them all a wry look. "Well, if it isn't the intrepid Rescue 2. And you even came bearing gifts."

"Hi, Mary!" Fitz drunkenly waved from his chair.

"Hi, Fitz. Good to see you made it a whole twelve hours before coming back. And Gary, it's always a pleasure. How's mom?"

"She'll be along shortly."

Nurse Mary looked at Rodell. "Push Fitz into Club Med. One of the C.N.A.'s will clean him later."

Club Med was actually an alcove where the drunks were stored. Rodell had seen as many as ten in there facing the wall, sleeping, peeing themselves, and worse. Four early risers had already checked in, completely wrecked. Alcoholics found on the street used to go to jail until one of them died from a diabetic event, so now everyone went to the Emergency Room.

Nurse Mary, who was old enough to be Lt. Doneen's mom, was the wrong person to piss off. As gatekeeper for the ER, she could turn a five minute drop-off into a thirty minute nightmare if mistakenly provoked. No stranger to hard work and thankless situations, she looked out for the firemen that looked out for her—mainly complete patient histories, EKG strip, IV, and properly dosed medications to start. She was entering both patients into her computer as Lt. Doneen looked at the chaos over her shoulder and said, "You on a twelve-hour?"

"Eighteen. I'm covering for Alicia tonight."

"Sucks to be you."

"Careful, Mikey, I just told you I was gonna be here all damn day."

"My bad." He put an arm around her shoulder as she typed. "We can't be hating. Not if I'm gonna be spending the whole day here."

"That busy?"

"Left the station at ten after seven and haven't seen it since. Row's gonna kill me if I don't let him get an ice coffee before our next run."

"Good idea." She signed his paperwork and handed it back. "Bring one back for me and I'll be your buddy forever."

"Done."

"Talked with Timmy on Rescue 1 this morning. He told me today's the day ..."

"Isn't it incredible? Out of all the fuck ups, the only guys who did their jobs right are the ones about to get drilled?"

"It won't come to that."

"Yeah? I'll bet their math says different. Why not jam up two firemen instead of admitting the police dispatch screwed up, the fire dispatch made it worse, and the city should be absolved of it all?"

"You're too young to be this cynical."

Rodell appeared with a fresh sheet for the stretcher and IV supplies from the stock room. He said, "Dude. If you love me, you won't call back in service until we hit a Dunkin'."

"Hell yeah, kid. Let's do it. See ya, Mary."

"Don't hurry back," she said as they headed for the door. "We're already busy enough!"

They were loading the stretcher when their radios crackled. *"Fire Alarm to Rescue 2?"*

"Seriously?" Rodell punched the side of the truck. "I'm trying hard not to lose it."

Lt. Doneen toggled his shoulder-mic. "Rescue 2's on, Fire Alarm. We'll be clearing Memorial momentarily. You gotta run for us?"

"Please kill me."

"Row, if it's nonsense, we'll take thirty seconds to stop for coffee. Relax."

"Roger, Rescue 2, start responding with Engine 4 to 516 Broadway for a child allergic reaction, possible airway involvement."

"Roger."

Fire Alarm hit the alert tone and said, *"That's Rescue 2 and Engine 4, 516—that's 5-1-6—Broadway, 3rd floor, for a child allergic reaction, possible airway involvement ..."*

By protocol, the dispatch was repeated twice more but wasn't necessary. Few things got the Fire Department moving faster than anything involving a kid. Lt. Doneen braced on the dash as Rodell punched it and said, "Guess we ain't stopping for coffee."

"At this rate, lunch will be a luxury."

Ahead, the screaming rescue cleaved traffic in two.

***

An hour later, they returned to the station and caught sixty minutes peace. With only two rescues for 80,000 citizens, 82,000 if the number of illegal immigrants was estimated, slow days were the exception. In fact, since they each did over 5200 runs a year, both trucks were in the top twenty busiest rescue companies on the whole east coast.

After lunch, the engine and ladder guys did the dishes since the rescue was barely there. In the bay, Rodell leaned against the truck and smoked while scrolling through his phone. Lt. Doneen was inside re-stocking medications when Rodell called out, "Well, lookee here. If it ain't Doctor Chaos."

A red unmarked department sedan came flying into the station. Lonnie Chance, a twelve-year veteran with all of it spent on rescue, gave them both the finger. In his mid-thirties, he still wore his now graying hair high and tight. A former Army Ranger combat medic, Chance was now unofficially in charge of the entire EMS division.

"The Bee-Gees," Chance said, poking fun at the Brothers Grimm. "What a slaughter-fest. You guys're getting absolutely smoked today."

"What's up, Lonnie?" Rodell slapped his hand.

"Car 6." Lt. Doneen poked his head out the side door. "How goes the battle?"

"You tell me. As much as I love you guys, this ain't no social call."

"You hear anything yet?"

"Negative." Chance scanned the massive equipment bay for eavesdroppers. "1500 hours is a hard clock. Personally, I don't think there's anything to worry about. The board has to know that if they smoke you guys, the press is gonna ride this story for days. Everyone loses."

"Maybe."

"Maybe nothing. Besides, the reason David versus Goliath's been around for a million years is because no one ever roots for Goliath."

"Politics, Lonnie, makes us completely expendable."

"Damn, dude." Rodell took one last inhale before snapping away his butt. "I really hate it when you say shit like that."

"Why?"

"Because it's usually true."

"Not this time," Chance said. "Believe me when I tell you—people're watching. As they should be. If this ruling becomes precedent it effects everyone. My counterparts in ten other departments, including Providence, tell me they'll march a thousand firemen down to the Board of Health."

"Well ..."

"Listen, this is also a good news/bad news situation. Chief just told me if you guys get exonerated or placed on probation you finish the shift. But if they recommend suspension or worse, your licenses will be immediately pulled. You'll both be sent home. Like by 3:05."

Rodell turned and punched the truck a half dozen times. Then he looked at his hand because it hurt. "I'm about ready to just walk out of this motherfucker altogether."

The alert tone hit and Fire Alarm said, "*Attention Rescue 2 and Engine 1. Still alarm. 170 West Avenue. Meet the police on-scene for a victim of assault …*"

"Great." Rodell re-slung his radio and headed for the driver's seat. "Looks like someone just got their ass beat on a perfectly sunny day."

Chance called out, "I'll be in touch by three o'clock."

"Roger that." Lt. Doneen grabbed the microphone. "Rescue 2's responding."

"*Rescue 2 responding at 1325.*"

"Headed for the ghetto," Rodell said. "Exactly where we belong."

"Right? Always quality runs in the ghetto."

District 1, like Districts 3, 4, and 5, had massive triple and quadruple-decker homes originally built a century before to house thousands of workers. But with the mills closed, and no fire-stops between floors, these giant houses now turned into massive conflagrations if not vigorously attacked.

District 1 was across the highway from District 2. After years of bad blood between neighborhoods, rival gangs defended either side of I-95 like warring clans dropping bodies.

Rescue 2 arrived to find the guys from Engine 1 huddled over a crying woman.

"Damnit," Rodell said, parking in front of the engine. "I hate domestics."

"Me too." Lt. Doneen grabbed the microphone. "Rescue 2's on scene."

"*Roger, Rescue 2, on scene at 1328.*"

Lieutenant Walls of Engine 1 corralled them as they exited the truck. In a hushed voice, he said, "She says the boyfriend got home an hour ago. He's been cracking out for days. She offered to make him something to eat. Then she says he lost it for no reason and literally beat her unconscious. When she woke up, he was raping her."

"Jesus." Lt. Doneen snuck a peak at her but the blanket was pulled over her head. "Where're the cops?"

"Dunno."

"Rescue 2 to Fire Alarm," he said into his radio. "Are police en route?"

"That's a roger, Rescue 2."

Lt. Doneen turned to Lt. Walls. "Timing wise, this just happened?"

"Yeah. She says after she got out of the duct tape, she actually chased him off with his own gun."

"Good for her. Too bad she didn't just fucking smoke him."

Rodell approached her and squatted down to make eye contact. "Hey, darling, my name's Jimmy but everyone calls me Row. Can we just get you into the rescue? Check you out? Maybe wash up some of those cuts?"

She might have been Hispanic, but with all the bruises and tear-stained make-up, it was impossible to tell.

Rodell helped her to her feet. "What's your name?"

"Maria." She wiped her eyes, and, like most rape victims, wanted nothing to do with any of the males suddenly around her.

Because of this, Lt. Doneen turned to Lt. Walls and said, "We got this, lou. You guys can clear."

"Listen, Mikey ..." Walls shook his hand. "We're all pulling for you guys. Fuck the Board of Health."

"Appreciate that, L-T." Lt. Doneen helped her into the truck. "See you at the next one."

Inside, they threw on the heat and got vital signs. Because of the sexual assault, they did not clean her face, hands, or do a thorough trauma assessment since the hospital would perform a full rape-kit. Rodell draped another blanket around her on the stretcher.

"He's still here," she quietly said through the tears. "His boys will try to hide him."

"What's his name?" Rodell asked, removing the blood pressure cuff.

"I can't tell you that."

"Maria, I know you're scared, but you chased this guy off with his own piece."

"There are too many of them."

A policeman poked his head in the side door. "Whaddaya got?"

Outside, Lt. Doneen briefed the cop. "Apartment 16. She says the gun's on the table. Boyfriend sounds like a gangbanger because she keeps talking about all his boys."

The cop furiously scribbled on a notepad. "She won't give him up, huh?"

"Negative. Listen, I gotta get her out of here. Headed to Memorial. You cool with that?"

"Yeah. I'll have the sex crimes detectives head straight there."

Lt. Doneen got back into the truck and told Rodell, "Let's roll."

Minutes later they swept into the ER. Rodell grabbed the microphone. "Rescue 2's off at Memorial."

"*Roger. Rescue 2 off at Memorial, 1355.*"

"One more hour to go!" Rodell shouted, but his partner was not amused.

They wheeled Maria in to where nurse Mary awaited their report. Mary consoled Maria and immediately put her into a private room. When Mary returned to her computer, she found an ice coffee from the cafeteria beside it. She pinched Lt. Doneen's cheek and said, "You are a God, Mikey Doneen."

"I'm a man of my word. Who knows? This might be the last time we ever see each other."

"Don't say that!"

Mrs. Janowski and her diabetic son Gary were readying to leave when she saw Lt. Doneen. "Everything's fine, Lieutenant. Isn't that great news?"

"It sure is. You look a lot better, Gary. How you feeling?"

"Hopefully good enough not to pass out behind the wheel on the way home." He clapped Lt. Doneen on the shoulder. "Thanks again."

"No worries."

Mrs. Janowski kissed him on the cheek. "You guys are the best. Thank you so much."

"Fire Alarm to Rescue 2?"

Lt. Doneen told the Janowskis, "I gotta take this. Have a good day." He walked away and said into his radio, "Rescue 2, go."

"Rescue 2, when you clear Memorial, Car 2 would like you to report downtown."

Lt. Doneen looked at Mary. "They're taking us off the road. Maybe they already got the call?" He clicked the microphone. "Rescue 2 copy."

Rodell approached with fresh linen for the stretcher. "Unbelievable. Let's just get this over with."

You're right."

Mary hugged them. "There's no need to worry. Trust me. Pawtucket needs the Bee-Gees sweeping up the east side."

They smiled, said good-bye, and took the drive to headquarters.

***

The whole thing had started with a frantic 911 call six weeks before. Shots were fired on Makin Street, but police dispatch put the call out for Aiken Street. Even worse, fire dispatch thought the police said Bacon Street, so everyone went to the wrong place. By the time personnel arrived on-scene ten minutes after the shooting, an eighteen-year-old kid was circling the drain. The gunshots to his leg and arm were bad enough, but the collapsed lung and internal bleeding caused Rodell and Lt. Doneen to race him to R.I.H. There, the doctors immediately pronounced him dead.

Now, at three o'clock, Assistant Chief Rice, Battalion Chief Switzer, Lonnie Chance, Lt. Doneen, and Rodell were gathered around a speaker-phone at headquarters. After all the introductions, the head of the Ambulance Advisory Board went through ten minutes of legalese before shocking the room.

"It is our direct finding that medical negligence and patient neglect form a case for dereliction of duty—"

"The guy was dying!" Rodell looked ready to throttle the speaker-phone.

"The chest tube was outside your scope of practice, and violates your licensure with the state—"

Lt. Doneen tried to remain calm. "But it was a successful chest decompression. No one's argued otherwise. Without it, he had zero chance."

"Is this Lt. Doneen?"

"Yes."

"In your own sworn testimony, you said you saw a former partner, a Mr. Lonnie Chance, who, unlike either one of you, is a registered paramedic and combat medic fully qualified to attempt this procedure. He's not some fireman holding only a cardiac level license. Nonetheless, in your own words you said you watched him perform this intervention on two occasions. This, however, in no way allows either one of you to cut into the chest wall of a critically injured man—"

"This is incredible."

"Row, sit down. Take it easy." Lt. Doneen looked at the speaker-phone. "So you're suspending us because by the time two different dispatching errors were corrected, this guy was already as good as dead?"

"I'm afraid there's been some confusion. Suspensions were discussed but unfortunately the board has decided to permanently pull your EMT licenses."

Lt. Doneen looked at the Assistant Chief. "Without those, we're fired, right?"

I'm afraid so. But there is an appeals process—"

"That's it for me." Rodell stood up. "Fuck this. You're all just an incredible pack of pussies."

"Row!"

The door slammed closed. Lt. Doneen stared at the speaker. No one said a word. The speaker hummed.

"My partner's right." Lt. Doneen grabbed his radio. "This ain't about the truth or what's right, it's all about maximum CYA—Cover Your Ass."

"Mikey …"

Lt. Doneen headed for the door and paused. "Consider this a formal notification of my lawsuit against the city, the department, the chief, the mayor, the board of health, and anyone else my lawyer can add to the list."

Downstairs, Rodell was gathering his stuff out of the rescue. "I can't believe it."

"Me either. On the bright side, it's almost happy hour."

"Right? Maybe we can join Fitz at Asshole Tree."

"Sounds good."

"Hey …"

"Yeah?"

"I wouldn't change a thing."

Me neither." Lt. Doneen clapped him on the back. "Life and death, bro, life and death."

In the distance, the sirens of Rescue 1 echoed through the city.

An Uncommonly Common Event

by R.N. Chevalier

The young man behind the wheel looks in the rearview mirror. The lights from the bar fade away as the road bends slightly to the left. Several miles in the other direction is the town of Lincoln and several miles beyond that, the city of Providence. The direction he went, however, leads to the wooded, rural part of Rhode Island.

The road shining in the headlight beams hasn't changed for over an hour. The dark, moonless night envelops the world around the solo driver. It is two-thirty in the morning, and the southern New England back road seems to drone on endlessly. The last car passed nearly an hour earlier, yet despite the time, the driver is excited and awake, anticipating his meeting with one of M.I.T.'s top theoretical physicists in the morning.

His new theory that gravity is the by-product of the reaction between normal matter and dark matter as well as energy and dark energy, if correct, will help unify the theories of Albert Einstein. Tomorrow he starts working on the math formula, his first step to the Nobel Prize in physics. The purring of the brand new engine is hypnotic, and the "new car" smell is more intoxicating than the four beers and two shots he had done earlier. The climate control is set at seventy, and the cruise control is locked at seventy-five.

The driver takes the wheel with his knee and removes a small metal box from his vest pocket. He pops off the cover and places the box on the seat. He removes a cigarette lighter and a small metal pipe. He puts the pipe to his lips and lights the green weed packed in the chamber. He inhales slow and steady. He hears a familiar piano melody start on the radio and turns up the volume. "The dark side's callin', now nothin' is real. She'll never know just how I feel." He exhales and sings along. "From out of the shadows, she walks like a dream. Make me feel crazy, make me feel so mean. Ain't nothin' gonna save you from a love so blind. Slip to the dark side and cross that line. On the dark side, oh yeah. On the dark side, oh yeah." He takes another long, slow hit from the pipe, then puts the pipe and lighter back in the case, as John Cafferty and the Beaver Brown Band continues playing.

As he exhales, he notices a strange light just over his headlight beams. He regains control of his car with his hands and slows down, turning off the headlights to get a better look at the strange phenomenon. It appears to be a ring of light just sitting on the road several miles ahead of him. He looks off to the left and right of the ring, trying to find the source of the weird light. Seeing nothing, he looks above, then behind.

"What the hell is that?" he asks himself, bewilderment in his voice. "I'm not that stoned." He accelerates slowly, apprehensively, yet with excited anticipation. The vehicle moves forward, speeding up every second. Two minutes pass. The young driver takes another puff of his pipe. He now notices that the interior of the ring is large enough for his new car to fit into with room to spare. A sudden, overwhelming feeling of uneasiness overtakes him, as he realizes that the ring is causing his car to accelerate as it accelerates toward him. He looks down at his dashboard. He is going fifty-five miles an hour.

"Aahh!" he shouts out loud, as he slams both feet on the brake pedal. His reflexes take over as he grips the steering wheel tightly and locks his elbows, pushing his body tighter into the seat. Only now does he realize the song on the radio is playing much slower than it should be. The sound of the tires skidding on the asphalt drowns out the music in his ears. The car turns slightly sideways as it stops abruptly inside of the ring of light, blinding the young driver. He feels a sharp pain behind his eyes.

It takes some time before the brightly colored dots fade from his eyes. As his vision starts to clear and the pain fades away, he realizes his car is slowly rolling in the middle of the road. He swings

44

around, frantically trying to see where the light ring is and if there are any other cars approaching. Seeing a clear road, he puts his car in park and quickly gets out, trying a get a better look around. He is the sole being in sight in every direction. There is no sign of the ring of light.

"Something doesn't seem right," He says to himself as he looks around, calmer now. He thinks about it for several minutes. Not realizing any change, he gets back in his car. He turns the key but nothing happens. The lights inside and out are working fine, but the car refuses to start.

As the moonlight shines on the road ahead of him, he looks around. He still thinks something is out of place. He fumbles through the radio's preset stations, but none of them are broadcasting, not even static. As he hits the last selection and gets no signal, he looks up and his eyes open wide as the proverbial light bulb comes on over his head. He jumps out of the car.

"That's it!" he shouts into the night. He looks up at the brilliantly-lit night sky and a quarter moon hanging just above the tree line. There weren't any stars out! No stars, no moon, none of them! What the hell happened?

He gets back in the car, leaving the door open. He takes another hit from his pipe, trying to figure out what's going on. He waits five minutes, taking several more hits. Now, feeling more relaxed, he closes the door and tries the engine again. It starts with a loud roar. He starts driving slowly down the dark road. Five minutes pass silently, with only the sound of the engine to keep him company. In the distance he sees four horizontal lights approaching fast. He slows down and stays in the right lane.

"It's about time," he says to himself excitedly. He flicks his headlights on and off several times, as he comes to a stop, hoping the oncoming car will stop. Suddenly, the lights shoot up about twenty feet in the air as they get closer. He looks in amazement as the lights pass over him. He sticks his head out of the window, looking up at the lights. He sees a rectangle about twenty-five feet long by eight feet wide. "Hey!" a group of voices from the craft shout to him. He slowly gets out of his car. The craft does a tight circle, as he hears more shouts of greetings from it. It slowly lands on the ground beside him. It is a car with four figures in it. He stares in amazement, unable to speak. The doors open, and the four figures get out. They are only a few years younger than he is. There are two men and two women. They are smiling and happy. Their clothes are made of neither materials that he recognizes nor any familiar style. The four young people surround his GMC Envoy giggling with excitement.

"I'm Dave," the driver of the flying car says. "That's my girl, Rachel." He points to the girl who was in the passenger seat, who waves in greeting. "That's Travis and his girl Fran." He points to the two that were in the back seat.

"I'm Russ," The confused driver says.

"That is one awesome ride!" Dave says, seemingly ignoring Russ, who is mesmerized by the futuristic flying vehicle.

"You did a fantastic job restoring her," Travis says.

"Did you restore her yourself?" Fran asks.

"No...no," he stutters out. "I bought it new."

The four strangers start to laugh uncontrollably for a long few seconds.

"No, really," Dave says. "How long did it take for you to finish her? And where on this planet did you find the parts?"

"No, really," he answers. "I bought it new, like, two and a half months ago."

"What kind of drugs are you on?" Rachel asks. "I want some." The four laugh.

"Why would you say I'm on drugs?" Confusion fills his face.

"Because, man," Dave starts, "cars with gas combustion engines haven't been made in forty-five years."

"What the hell?" Russ asks rhetorically in disbelief. "What year is this?"

"What?" Dave asks, looking confused.

"What year is this?" Russ asks again with some panic in his voice.

"Two thousand seventy-one," Fran answers him. Russ's mouth hangs open as his mind tries to wrap around what he just heard. It takes a number of seconds.

"Why don't they make gas combustion engines anymore?"

"Look pal," Travis explains, "when the Chevalier Equation proofed out, those vehicles became obsolete."

"Chevalier Equation?" Confusion joins his panic. "What are you talking about? What equation?"

"Have you been under a rock?" Rachel asks.

"I think I have," he answers, "I feel like Rip Van Winkle."

"Who?" Fran asks.

"Never mind," he answers Fran then turns back to Rachel. "Please continue."

"Fifty years ago, this guy, Chevalier, came up with a formula in physics that made anti-gravity technology possible. Forty-five years ago, fossil fuel vehicles became obsolete, and we got the first flying cars." A smile spreads across the young driver's face.

"There are only a few hundred people in the country who still drive these," Dave tells him. "Fuel is like twelve bucks a gallon."

"That, along with the pollution restrictions of two thousand-forty makes it really expensive to drive," Travis adds.

"Tell me about your vehicle," Russ requests. "What's its propulsion? Its lift? Its range?"

"Hang on," Dave says with a slight laugh. "It's an Aurora Seven. It has eight RC-13 ion-flux lift engines and two, three-port Delta thrusters. It has limitless range."

"Unlimited range?" Russ is in disbelief. "What type of fuel does it use?"

"Fuel? No fuel," Dave says. "It is powered by the Tesla Energy Grid."

"Awesome," Russ says. "Can you take me for a ride?"

"Don't you have one?" asks Fran.

"No," he admits. "Where I'm from they haven't been invented yet."

"What did you say?" Travis asks.

"Never mind," Russ says. "I've figured it out. I pulled over and feel asleep. Now I'm dreaming."

"I don't think so, dude," Dave says.

"No matter," Russ says, convinced he's dreaming. "Can you take me for a ride? I'm going to enjoy this dream to the fullest."

"Lock your car up, and let's go," Dave says.

Russ locks the doors, and the five climb into the Aurora Seven, the man from the past riding shotgun. As the vehicle shoots upward, Russ grips the armrests tightly, inhaling loudly. The others laugh at his inexperience.

"Where would you like to go?" Dave asks.

"The coast?" Russ half asks. "Newport, maybe?"

"No problem," Dave says. "We'll be there in ten minutes."

"No shit?" Russ asks in amazement. A car-full of giggling is his answer.

The craft speeds along at an incredible rate, the landscape just a blur beneath them. It takes less than three minutes for the lights of Providence to become visible, as they approach the city over what Russ recognizes as Route 146 as it merges with Route 95.

Russ can see the Patriot statue standing atop the brightly lit Statehouse. He also sees the Providence Civic Center, now an abandoned hulk with a collapsed roof and crumbling walls.

"What happened to the Civic Center?" he asks.

"Blizzard of '65," Fran answers, "took out the rest of the Convention Center as well. Most of it was trashed by a fire the year before."

By the end of the brief conversation, the coastline of Newport is in view.

"What happened to the bridges?" he asks.

"Every bridge was disassembled," Rachel explains, "every bridge, every overpass, everything going over waterways."

The craft skims inches above the water, heading for a small island.

"Is that Block Island?"

"Yes, it is," Dave answers.

"Damn, this thing is fast."

"This is one of the slower models," Dave complains. "My parents won't let me get anything faster. 'Too dangerous,' they say."

"Maybe they're right," Russ replies, as he sees the edge of the craft clip the crest of a small wave as they circle around the island. It takes about a minute before they pass the lighthouse at Point Judith and get back over solid ground. They turn northwest over North Kingston and head toward Foster following the dark, wooded roads. Just over ten minutes pass, and the craft decelerates quickly and turns sharply to the right. It touches down gently just five feet from Russ's antique.

"Thank you for the look into the future," Russ says, as Rachel gets back into her seat. "Even if it's all just a dream, I got some good ideas."

"Have a good one," Dave says.

"I will," he assures them. "I just have to wake up."

The four give him one more curious look as they get back into the silver craft. It rises slowly into the air and speeds away silently. The young driver gets back into his car.

"Wake up, wake up," he says with determination, his eyes shut tightly. He opens one eye. Seeing that nothing's changed, he does it again. "Wake up, wake up, wake up." He opens his eyes after a few seconds. His face defines the disappointment he feels when, again, nothing's changed.

"I've got to find the ring of light," he says aloud, "but where?" He takes a long drag from his bowl and sits back in his seat, closing his eyes. His eyes fly wide open as he turns the key. The Envoy roars to life.

"I've got to head back toward Providence," he says to himself, as he turns his car around. He sits there for a moment, silently staring into the darkness ahead of him. He pushes hard on the accelerator. The car screams down the dark road, the driver smiling from ear to ear. His excitement about his meeting in a few hours is what, he believes, influenced his dream. The new ideas running in his head will only add to the conversation at M.I.T.

In the distance, he sees the ring of light he's searching for. He accelerates, excited to get back and reap the rewards of this discovery. As he enters the ring, a deafening sound fills his ears. Then, darkness.

The State Police cruiser pulls up to the Foster Police cruiser blocking the road.

"What's the story?" the officer in the car asks, seeing the twisted wreckage up ahead.

"Young guy, late night," the officer tells him. "He must have fallen asleep behind the wheel. He went head-on into the tractor-trailer."

"That sucks," the trooper says solemnly, looking at the ambulance parked down the street.

Sitting on the tailgate is the truck driver getting a gash on his forehead treated by an E.M.T.

"Strange thing," the Foster Police officer adds. "The truck driver said the guy looked like he was asleep, but he sped up and was smiling."

"Who was he?"

"No one important," the officer says, reading from his notepad. "Name is, was... Chevalier, Russ Chevalier."

Poetry

Destination Courage

By Helen Burke

Courage is a bicycle and I ride it

Up hill and down Dale , every day.

The wheels are my heart ticking away.

The handlebars are my soul

Steering so true, with your hand

In mine we two stay on course

And the sky becomes again blue.

Round and round the wheels of my

Heart sing as we climb the steep hills

There is no telling with courage how much

May be asked,

Courage smiles on the story that we two

Have told.

Let the bicycle of courage

Keep you well. Though you have some

Miles to go, the sun will come out.

And the compass of your love

Will Keep you brave.

Galilee

by Barbara Ann Whitman

What can be said of the sea
That has not already been written?
Its depths, its hues, its fickle waves;
Even the sun is smitten.

I leave my footprints in the sand
As I ponder life's intent.
The tide comes gently in, as if,
To wash away my discontent.

The fishing trawlers come and go
With hopeful gulls surrounding.
In the distance, low and deep,
A fog horn's call resounding.

At the jetty, eager children
Hunt for ocean treasures.
A plastic bucket filled with crabs;
Their faces filled with pleasure.

Across the inlet standing tall,
A sentinel of light
Marks the rocky coastline
From bricks of red and white.

My heartbeat slows, its cadence now
Is lilting with the tide.
My spirit finds a buoyancy
Only ocean can provide.

I say good-bye but linger there
For one last breath of sea
No doubt that my untroubled soul
Abides at Galilee.

Monuments at Blue Shutters

By Lawrence J. Krips

Found on my last visit
to this shore, the throne
awaits my arrival.
The sharply carved-out seat
of this boulder faces the sea.
Hidden from
the tourists behind me,
I sit on its
comfortable cushion
of moist sand.
The uneven armrests
give my body
a leeward tilt
as I survey the Atlantic
whose water washes
heat and sand from my feet.
The rhythm of the ocean
slaps the big rocks
in front of me;
placed there by the
children of the gods,
who, as young tourists,
discarded these toys,
now standing as ancient monuments
to their former presence.

Scanning the horizon,
earth's curvature is apparent.
Vessels, miles away,
sail on black water,
while more closely
dull foam and sharp reflections
dance in infinite patterns
to the newest songs of the wind.
The cadence of the perpetual
serves me as easily as those ships.
The sky has equal status here;
two masters emanating from that hinge.

I watch the world
with glacial patience
as my kingdom
erodes monuments.

Monday in Manville

By Dawn M. Porter

Trash cans strewn about the street,
plastic soldiers scattered by the wind.
Air brakes and the stench
of last week's sweet smells turned sour.

Triple deckers line quiet streets.
Warm sunshine beats down.
Gentle breezes cool.

A man in neon fleece pajamas
smoking a joint,
on a porch,
at high noon.

it's Monday in Manville.

The Seagulls Watch

By Frances L. O'Donnell

The *Seagulls* call to me,
Summoning me to the seashore,
near the bend of the rivers
edge, where fish land when caught.

I'm called with the intensity of a tsunami,
tearing down every inch of sand,
while the fish, awaiting their food, *lay* laundered.
Yet the fish might best linger and have some
purpose to not always be sought for the table.

The cries of the *Seagulls* pray to the others
to watch and hold tight.
It *felt* like the Rope of *life* was being scattered by means
of rapid velocity while the screeching of winds
and bellowing sounds of water, pounded the earth.

The *life* that once was filled with colorful dreams,
now look to gather the fruit from the magnificent trees.
But soon learn there is no more gathering fruit
as *life's* treasures have been *crushed* by the swift beating
of earth's *unwelcomed* visit

The land that once thrived with much splendor and grace,
remains swollen; lost of its pulse and luster, *life's* breath is
now injured with wounds of much reparation.
Where once erased, the hope is that *life's* gifts will no longer
be obliterated.

The *Seagulls* cry with horror of what they witnessed
and could not surpass but they held on to--- the thought,
that their cries were heard, their cries did warn.

Day's End
At Misquamicut Beach

By Jane F. Collen

The less fiery sun still
Hot kisses
Copper toned skin
between breezes its slant
Warms
Vibrant umbrella colors
Yellow

Tan mothers
Re-pack
Epic amounts of beach paraphernalia
Indispensable for so few hours in the sun; they
Call
Sand crabby children
Entrenched in freshly dug holes
Crying in denial of their departure

The blissful bouquet
of sunscreen and salt air
with a whiff of wild ocean
Promises
Advent of the
Quintessence of the day

Gulls
Circle
Wings stretched lazily
toward the slowly sliding sun
Caw
to the receding tide
Zero in
on toddler-abandoned treats
Boldly approach brightly colored blankets

The waves' rhythm
on the shore
Resonates
in my Heartbeat
White caps on sea green
Spray
Rocks; sparkles
Catch
Retreating sun

Boats
bearing puffy cloud sails
Race
across the green expanse
Heading for harbor

Sandpipers bravely
Storm
The water
Scurrying feet and fluttering wings
Peck
The shoreline
Abandon
Their plan

Retreating in formation
Eluding grasping waves

The lifeguard's whistle
Drops
The red and green flags

One more beautiful umbrella
Retired
for the night
Hot summer colors
Wrapped
to await
Another day's unfolding

My straw-like hair
Waves
across my face
To the departing families

Donning my sweatshirt, I
Relive
The sun-drenched days
so long ago
Endlessly playing
Water games
Sand writing
Drip castles
Laughing

Digging my heels into the sand, I
Revive
The dizzy-dazzling days
So short ago
Catching cold children

Changing them into dry suits
Feeding them
Building their castles
Loving them

Playing in the
Sun
As it
Slipped
Sand-like
Through my fingers
With the days

I
Remain
on the empty beach
Wrapped warmly
in my memories
Teased
by the wind
Toward tomorrow's horizon

The Moods of My Rhody Waters

By Deborah Katz

Its moods
   It rushes me.
It eludes
   It swirls me.
It exudes
   Life- topsy turvy.
Turning up
   Rolling up
Churning up
   Clams.
Whipping up
   Sands.
It masks its ferocity;
   Presents seemingly calm felicity.

You rush
   You gush
You envelop me with your salty, frothy foam so plush.

You speak to me in a roar
   As I ride you to the shore.
Each wave of yours unique: to be no more.

You lighten me
   With your buoyancy
Until I'm submerged from the force of your purge and I'm part of
thee.

Sometimes you are angry, Sea:
    When a child, you overwhelmed me.
Hurricane side effects turned the shore to a ditch, with undertow
wildly.

Calm Bonnet Shores it was before it changed,
    Until its height and depth did rearrange;
An outstretched hand pulled me out of danger's range.

In later years, it was with Narrow River too,
    Switching its course, its current was created anew;
My independent motion bid adieu.

Carrying me toward the rocks in the bay,
    An outstretched arm impeded my way,
To save me that day.

Quirks and Quahogs

By Debbie Kaiman Tillinghast

Rhode Island is the smallest state, but big on quirks and flavor
We've given birth to many foods with tastes for you to savor

The scent of roasting coffee wafts through the morning air,
It's Rhody's favorite flavor, you'll find coffee everywhere
There's hot in cups, and in ice cream, in syrup for our milk,
Churn ice cream, milk and syrup for a cabinet smooth as silk.
The sign says New York System, but they're really Rhody's own,
Wieners in a soft white bun, you can't have just one alone
Smothered in a brown meat sauce, essential for the works
Lined twelve along a cook's long arm, another Rhody quirk
Add, mustard, onions, relish, don't forget the celery salt
With a glass of coffee milk, it's a match you will exalt

When days are hot and sultry, find the truck that's green and white
Del's Lemonade is slushy ice and tastes sweet-tangy bright
Looking for a sandwich large? A grinder it will be
For in R-I a submarine, sails beneath the sea
Doughboys are a classic, made with pizza dough we fry
Add a sugar sprinkle for a blissful treat to try
We don't want a party, without our square cut Pizza Strips
A thick moist crust with seasoned sauce, makes all kids lick their lips.
Calamari in Rhode Island are served a unique way,
With banana peppers and hot sauce, eat them by the bay.
There are hard shell clams called Quahogs, to keep us all replete
And steamers that stay hidden, in the mud flats 'neath your feet

But summer in the Ocean State, the quahogs reign supreme
You'll find them in some tasty treats, perhaps you've never seen
Grind them up and add potatoes, simmer in a briny broth
Ignore the milk you won't need it, that's for chowders further north
Clam cakes are essential to keep your chowder company,
Brown and crispy outside, and inside you'll taste the sea
Balls of soft and sticky dough swim in bubbling fat
Laced with bits of chewy clams, now what do you think of that?
Stuffies are a favorite, the shells their baking dishes
Chop clams, then add bread crumbs and spice and even sausages

On May Day all across the state, May Breakfasts you will find
Since 1867 a tradition we've refined
The smell of bacon draws them in, the line goes out the door
Churches have prepared a feast of Johnny Cakes and more
Thin and crisp East of the bay, West they're soft inside
For this you scald the corn meal first, this Newport can't abide.
You'll see May baskets trimmed with frills, filled with fudge and
flowers
Take one to your friends nearby to brighten many hours
Leave it on their doorstep, then knock and run to hide
Wait for them to find you, and invite you back inside

Explore Rhode Island North to South, walk miles of sandy shore
Sample all our quirky flavors, they will leave you wanting more.

The Storm of the 13th State - Confusion

by Christie O'Neil Harrison

Listening to the icy
 Wet snow-slush
Beating upon my
 Window panes

In our Little Rhody
 World
everything stops
for this snowstorm
Except ...

Not really.

The sirens whine
The plows drive on.

Power is out.
I am cut off from
the rest of the world

Cocooned.

Suddenly, with a beep
 and a flicker
Electricity once again
 courses through the

veins of this old
urban home.

For 48 hours
the National Weather Service
predicted a blizzard for us

And, dutifully, the
Rhode Islanders flocked
To keep their shelves stocked
With bread, milk, and sundries such.

Mother Nature, she had
a different plan
Oh, the snow it came
But then turned to rain.

Tomorrow, it will be back to work.

Essays &
Non-Fiction

Bittersweet

by Edward Taylor

They say hindsight is twenty-twenty, and the older I get the more I seem to relate to the old adage. My teenage self would scoff at the nostalgic mess I have become. A rapidly aging man sitting on the steps of India Point Park staring out at the harbor, reliving all the fond memories that I took for granted. The years of live music, art festivals, quirky food trucks, or simply lying in the grass and staring up at the sky. I met the love of my life, broke my first bone, and snuck my first beer all within the confines of the tiny park tucked away in one of the most underrated cities on the eastern seaboard. The first beer and the broken bone occurred on the same night, of course.

I was the cliché. A punk kid who thought the world owed him a favor. A youth spent fantasizing about what life would be like when I left the quaint little state I called home. Like every other twenty-something I wanted to move far away, and assumed life would be infinitely more interesting once I put down roots in one of the country's, "real," cities. One day I'd look back and laugh at my peculiar old town, and the only time I'd ever return was when I was dragged back home for the odd family gathering. To put it bluntly, I was quite the little snot.

Sure, the taxes are high and the politicians are corrupt, but there's something about Rhode Island. I've never known a more pessimistic, and yet oddly proud, group outside of my home town. Rhode Islanders are typically the first people to mock their tiny corner of the country, but would gush over the most trivial detail that reminded them of home.

It's a never-ending list of contradictions, in the best way possible. Our politicians will take the microphone at political conventions and with a straight face claim we're home to the best restaurants, but the state's most iconic meal consists of sausages coated in fly sauce affectionately referred to as, "gaggers," pounded back with coffee flavored milk. We have one of the most academically minded capitols in the country, and yet our accent would give the professor in *Pygmalion* a stroke. We live in the smallest state in the union, where we can be nearly anywhere within an hour, but we look at driving one town over as an arduous endeavor.

Rhode Island is tough place to define, which is probably one of the main reasons I grew to love the state. It has a certain personality you can't find anywhere else. Not even our governor could adequately sum it up in a catchy tourism slogan. Everything I once rolled my eyes at became a point of pride. In my misguided youth I hated the fact that I hailed from the smallest state in the country, but now I wouldn't have it any other way. It was one hell of a place to grow up, and looking back I don't know how I didn't realize that at the time.

One of my earliest childhood memories was eating at Champlins, one of the many seafood joints our humble little state has to offer. My parents stopped to enjoy fried clams while watching the ships pass by just beyond the shore. I was more interested in the seagulls walking on top of the tarp over our table. Only the bottom of their feet could be seen on the other side of the blue fabric, and I found it to be one of the funniest things in the world. I couldn't control my laughter at the many pairs of webbed feet scurrying about randomly in search of their next meal. I doubt the tarp is still there all these years later.

My father is a massive fishing fanatic, and naturally my fondest memories with him revolved around the water. The time he got a new boat and took me out on the bay for the first time, I sat in a mild panic as the waves picked up and rocked us about fearing we would capsize when in reality we were perfectly safe. The time we went clam digging and I was fascinated by the abundance of tiny crabs that appeared out of nowhere once I dug my rake through the mud. All the summer nights we spent camping on the beach. My dad giving me the mattress he kept under the covered bed of his nearly tank sized truck, while he slept in the cramped front seat despite that I was all of three feet tall at the time. He still complains about the seat belt digging into his ribs to this day.

I'd fantasize about the mansion that overlooked my favorite beach. First, I imagined that the ghost of a woman who lost her beloved at the hands of the sea haunted the halls. She was the wife of a fisherman who could be seen overlooking the shore late at night as if she was still waiting for her husband to return. When I was old enough to realize a fisherman could never afford the house, I created the story of a retired bootlegger who hid away his illegitimate fortune within the guarded walls of the mansion.

Reality was far more depressing, of course. Eventually the house was sold to a pop star that uses it occasionally as their vacation home. The state isn't known for its paparazzi, but that didn't stop a few die-hard fans from trying to swim onto her beach. It wasn't the fact a pop star owned the home that I found depressing, but rather that the singer was only one year my senior and their second home costs more than what I'll make in my lifetime.

Like most Rhode Islanders, it seems all of my most memorable childhood moments occur a stone's throw from the ocean. Each summer my grandmother would rent a tiny beach house for a week or so, and all of us would gather in the glorified pillbox. I'd spend hours under the deck playing in the sand digging trenches or whatever else my young mind could come up with. My mother would read while taking in the sunlight, and my father would always keep one eye on the water. If there were even a hint of fish breaking the surface, he'd tap into a hidden athleticism few of us knew existed. I'd never seen someone run through sand as proficiently as my dad when there were bluefish feeding just off shore. An impressive feat when you consider he was also carrying a cumbersome salt-water fishing rod.

My mother had her fair share of heart attacks when it came to watching me play on the beach. The time my dad ran off to catch fish, knowing I was perfectly safe under the deck, but my mom leaving the beach house not knowing where I had gone; when I fell face first through a sandcastle and I began to chew the mouthful of sand that I had nearly inhaled. My mother forced me to spit it out before I ground my baby teeth to stubs, trying not to obviously laugh as I chased down the seagull that managed to steal my breakfast screaming, "Give me back my donut!" Luckily I wasn't successful, or my mother would have had another moment of panic, as I probably still would have eaten it knowing me.

Despite all these fond memories, I eventually grew to hate the beach. I detested the sensation and smell of sunscreen on my skin, and with my fair complexion there wasn't any wiggle room. Either I practically submerged myself in a vat of the stuff, or I was forced to stick to the shadows like a vampire on summer holiday. The little Portuguese blood I have couldn't offset my mostly French and Irish background. A shiver went up my spine whenever seaweed touched my leg, and I hated baking on a boat in the middle of the water on a summer day.

Of course there's more to the state than the beaches, but that was the beginning of the turn. My teens were fast approaching and I thought I knew best. Somehow I got it into my head that a city wasn't truly a city unless it had a subway. Where that nonsensical notion came from would be anyone's guess. When college came around, most of my schools were far beyond state lines, and I looked at it as the perfect opportunity to escape. In the end financial realities forced me to stay local, which didn't help my pessimistic attitude towards the state I felt I couldn't escape from.

While I enjoyed the odd concert, the wealth of cultural opportunities was lost on me. I'd scoff that one the state's most famous events was people literally sitting around watching bowls of fire hovering just a few inches over the water. I was first in line at the club, but never at any of the smaller scale venues that made up the backbone of Rhode Island's vibrant arts scene. I was a kid who claimed to enjoy culture, while not taking advantage of the creative capitol. My friends didn't help my outlook. One by one they'd come back after failing to cut it in the bigger cities, referring to the state as, "the magnet," in a condescending tone.

I had missed out on so much by the time I grew up and realized just how good I had it. I was lucky to be born in a state with such a diverse palate of opportunities to choose from. My entire life was spent a stone's throw away from ocean and yet I had all the cultural offers you'd find in the, "real," cities I held in such misguided regard. The beauty of Newport and Block Island were only a ferry ride away. That Waterfire takes on a whole new meaning when you share it someone special, and not your pretentious peers who looked at the event as an excuse to walk around aimlessly mocking the calming music.

Maybe Rhode Island being, "the magnet," wasn't really a bad thing? In retrospect I think it speaks volumes. Despite all the things my friends said about the state they claimed to hate, every single one of them came back. They could have gone anywhere else, and yet here they were complaining with me over coffee on Wickenden Street as if they never left. I think deep down we all knew our home was something special, and while other cities were great you still found yourself missing Providence. Now it was my turn to find out.

"Honey, the cab is here." My wife called from some distance, breaking me out of my train of thought.

I turned to face towards the bridge that led to the east side of Providence, the neighborhood we called home since college. My wife's red hair blew in the wind, and she seemed exhausted after a day of packing. I did most of the legwork of course. Her due date was only two months away, and the pregnancy had begun to take its toll. Even after three years I don't know how I convinced her marry to me. She was out of my league in every way. Her fancy Brown University diploma far outclassed my own, and strangers had literally taken it as a joke when they heard her introduce me as her husband on my less well-dressed days.

"Be right there baby." I replied with a warm smile.

She slowly made her way back towards the cab as I turned to take in the view one last time. I tried to commit it all to memory: the young couples lounging on the hill overlooking the harbor like my wife and I had done countless times before, the father and son fishing by the edge of the water, and the wind turbines that I once hated but grew to love slowly spinning in the distance.

Unfortunately my teenage dreams had eventually come true, years after I had stopped wishing they would. Despite growing to love my quirky little corner of the world, the big job came looking for me. It was an opportunity I'd be a fool to turn down. I was excited to have landed my dream job. Working in politics had been my dream, but I wish it didn't come at such a cost. For better or worse in a few short hours I'd board a plane for Washington D.C., only to return for the family events that I once dreaded would bring me back. Except now I found myself looking forward to them.

When I first learned my wife was pregnant I started to look forward to sharing all the same experiences I had as a kid. I was excited to be the quirky dad who takes their kid to the beach to build sand forts and go on adventures. Introduce my children to all the diverse experiences our little state has to offer, and end the night by gathering the family at Waterplace Park to watch the fire and simply enjoy each other's company. To find out if Champlins still has that blue tarp.

It's funny how time changes your perspective. I didn't want to leave. It took far too long to realize just how lucky I had been to grow up in such a special corner of the world. Hopefully I'd take a little piece of home with me wherever I end up. Like I said, there's just something about Rhode Island.

Friend

by Jessica M. Colette

T hrough my child eyes, you were large and intimidating. At the thought of meeting you, I felt scared, yet the excitement of the unknown that coursed through me was electric. Though everything about you was foreign, I was hopeful our differences would unite us as fast friends. Or was that wishful thinking? Could I be dreadfully wrong?

That was the summer of 1985. There wasn't anything particularly different about that summer, other than the fact that everything I knew to be real was shifting. The axis of my world was pointing due south. I watched the pastures and mountains fade into the distance through the rear window of our wood paneled station wagon. As the landscape's grandeur faded, my grip on the tan leather-like interior intensified until my knuckles turned ghostly white. It was clear I was beginning a new adventure and there was no chance of turning back.

My parents did their best to ease my anxiety. They assured me my new *friend* was just a few hours away. Though I believed them completely and knew they held every word they said to me to be truth, it was this new *friend* they referred to that I questioned. Would this *friend* be one to fill only a season of my life like which I was leaving behind, or would they be a lifelong companion? This was a question no child or parent could answer. It was a story only time could tell.

In retrospect, I can't say this new *friend* and I hit it off immediately. We were quite different, more than I anticipated. To even think about beginning a friendship, first, I had to understand our differences. Secondly, you had to accept mine.

To start, you spoke with a funny accent. I couldn't hear it all the time, just in certain words and phrases. At first, it made me laugh, until I quickly learned to embrace the nuance of our shared English language. If I'm honest, you were right; it is so much easier to turn *r's* into *a's* and vice versa. You also offered me food I had never tried before. Wow, who knew cold pizza with no cheese could taste so unbelievably good? But, it was the day you led me to the ocean that changed my life. When I wiggled my toes in the supple sand and allowed the frothy coolness of the waves to wash them clean, was the moment I knew our friendship was one that would last.

Allowing myself to see our differences, learning through patience to embrace them, with time, we could both fully grasp and appreciate the many things we have in common. After all, being a bit lazy with grammar, enjoying tasty food, and having an unquenchable love of the sea, are the commonalities that sealed our relationship.

Over the years, as we grew up together, we never drifted apart. We have both matured through change – some good, some not, all necessary –allowing us to say we've lived. Now, through the lens of maturity, my eyes see you for who you were then and who you are now.

You're a little less intimidating than you once were and a lot smaller than you once seemed. You still speak a little funny, but then again, so do I. The pizza (or should I say *pizzer*) you introduced me to has morphed into a craving, a hunger, I cannot ignore. But out of all you've shown me, the thing closest to my heart is when you lead me. You don't stop until you've brought me back to my favorite spot. It's the one you introduced me to in my youth, many years ago. It's where the sand embraces my weary bones with an acquainted touch and the waves sing to me in a familiar voice I know is yours.

Quonnie

by Susan Letendre

Quonnie felt more like home than home. We traveled down each summer from north of Hartford to spend a couple of weeks to a month in Quonochontaug, a beach community in Charlestown, Rhode Island. During what was then a long car ride, games of "Beaver" (or "spotting station wagons") would finally cede right of place as we raised our noses and stretched our necks out the car windows to be first to smell the salt in the air. Soon after, we would pull into one of the picnic areas along Route 1. These groves were built by the Civilian Conservation Corps, probably Company 141, housed just up the road at Burlingame State Park. They had crafted the benches and fireplaces out of the granite that litters the state, stone that, in another era, had been stacked into fences to clear the land for planting. Other travelers lit the fireplaces to grill hamburgers and hot dogs, but my family was in a hurry…. our beach was waiting. So, it was simple sandwiches and sweet pickles for us.

Those early years were magical. The Sea Breeze Inn, where we met the same people, the same weeks each year, felt like a family reunion. There was a young couple, newlyweds the first year, whose names were the same as my parents, Francis and Shirley. They adopted me when I was five, taking me to Misquamicut Beach where a Ferris wheel ride made me throw up. I didn't get over the humiliation until the next year.

My memory tells me that all the cooks were round, pink, and smiling. They served us fluffy omelets and stacks of thin crepes, along with fresh-squeezed raspberry juice for breakfast. Dinners ended with tortes or tarts with whipped top cream from the unhomogenized milk of the cow that lived up the street. The corridors and rooms of the Inn were permeated with the scents of bubbling butter, melted sugar, warm fruit, and salt air.

In the evenings, we youngsters lounged on sofas, plopped down at card tables, or pressed close at the piano. Many of us learned to shuffle and deal or play "Chopsticks" for the first time there. We played cards, sang, shared jokes, and laughed ourselves silly and tired. On the porch, adults rocked and talked into the dusk. At a designated hour, a few of the teenage boys would drive out to the Hitching Post up on Route 1, returning laden with bags of hot clam cakes. Soon, we full-bellied and greasy-fingered young ones would be shepherded off for a quick wash and a tuck into bed.

Just across the lawn was the dance hall. The original one had blown down in the '38 hurricane, and this one was rebuilt by the Nurmi family in 1940. It was a solid beamed building with windows on three sides, and a stone hearth on the fourth. The wood smelled of pine tar and, of course, salt. On Friday evenings, the whole community came for dances, the music provided by fiddlers and an accordion player. But, on the rainy day that we snuck in, there was the magic Wurlitzer. We kids would play the single records and marvel at the cascading lights and complex mechanism. My favorite song was the exotic "Take Me Back to Constantinople." Late evenings, when we children were asleep, our parents and the young couples would step across the dewy grass to the dance hall. In my imagination they sway and sing softly in one another's' ears their favorite romantic melodies.

Before we kicked off our sheets in the morning, a grey blanket would come in from the ocean and cover the Inn. Early mornings were always foggy. But when a day *stayed* socked in, the men would slosh out in hip boots onto the tidal flats, clam rakes on shoulders, to fill buckets with the littlenecks they sucked up from the mud. The women and children would go out berrying, returning with stained fingers and baskets of fruit. There would be berry juices for breakfast the next day. My favorite was the sweet-tangy raspberry juice, but there was also blueberry, currant, and blackberry.

One particular morning, when I was old enough to read "oatmeal" on the menu posted the evening before, I feigned a stomachache. When I peeked out of our room an hour later, Mrs. Nurmi swept me up and sent me through the swinging door of the kitchen. There, a cook, elbow-deep in pastry, paused from her task long enough to griddle me a stack of cakes. And, because my stomach was upset (hah!), she gave me a Coca Cola! I sat at the flour-dusted, wide-boarded table, in the midst of those rich, bubbling smells, eyes like sand dollars, watching her wield the clacking wooden rolling pin, turning out white wonders to brown in the oven. Seven-year-old heaven. And perhaps the making of a future baker. (In a much later year, I opened a bakery in Wakefield: Suzanne's Creative Pastries. People told me often that the bakery reminded them of their grandmother's kitchen. It was the smells, of course, as nobody's grandmother had a stainless-steel and polished-slate kitchen with huge Blodget ovens.)

1960 brought the twelfth year of my life, and the death of old Mrs. Nurmi. Nurmi means "pasture" in Finnish, and she had been as calm and nurturing as one. I was told that her family disagreed about what to do with the Inn, and left it too long. It fell to neglect and vandalism, and had to be razed.

The property was sold, and eventually a family built a house there and their guesthouse incorporated the dance hall. It is odd, indeed, for me to drive down West Beach Road and see the dance hall, but no Inn. I don't think there is a sprig left of the berry patches or currant bushes. I read there is a Wurlitzer, though, or at least some make of jukebox.

When the Inn was gone, we spent a summer on the Cape, but Quonnie drew us back. So, beginning the next year, we rented a cottage there each summer. We kids were old enough then to head down to the beach on our own. The Quonnie shore is strewn with boulders, dredged up by an advancing glacier 10,000 years ago and abandoned there when it retreated. The giant rocks define the beaches and their communities to this day, from Blue Shutters to the Quonochontaug Breachway, as they surely did when the indigenous people made their summer camp there, planting their crops and feasting on an abundance of shellfish after a lean winter. Backing the ocean was a chain of salt ponds, each one a sanctuary from the roar of tides on the other side of the dunes. In my time, both birds and people took rest in them.

One year, it must have been '65 or '66, Alan, a summer friend, returned from France with a smattering of continental ways. He harvested mussels from below the low tide marks on those boulders, and that night, steamed them open. Quite a few guests were reluctant to indulge. "Are you *sure* these are edible, Alan? How can you know they're the same kind the French eat?" No one got sick though. But within another five years, nary a mussel big enough to eat could be found on Quonnie Beach for overharvesting.

These were happy times, we and our parents being free from the obligations of everyday work and schedules. They could get up when they wished, head to the beach, swim and sunbath, returning only to make sandwiches for hungry children. It was a time away for us children, too.

I remember one morning in particular. I must have been fourteen, an angst-filled age for the dreamy child that I was. I had awoken and dressed, grabbed toast, and headed to the beach.

I felt an affinity with the fog that was still low over the cottages. In my memory, I walk along the road to the beach through the greyness, along the row of telephone wires where dozens of mourning doves sit cooing. I think they coo because they are sad, as I am, in this fog. But under the sadness is a stirring. The fog begins to swirl and lift, and, in great feathery plumes, flies out to sea. As if in a second, the day alights, the sun first glowing on the airborne droplets, and then burning through. I see the blue of the sea, Block Island, and perhaps, on this clear day, the tip of Long Island. The sadness flees with the fog, and my heart takes wing.

These early memories brought me back for college at the University of Rhode Island, and then, after stints in Austria, Massachusetts, and New Hampshire, to live here permanently. There is still no place on this earth that is so much "home." And it began, for me, with Quonnie.

Running on Empty

by Joanne Perella

A ll around me anxious runners were packed in as tight as sardines. In the distance, I could see the first group of runners begin as the gun went off. The wait for our group was just five minutes or so, but I was impatient to begin. Next to me, a young woman bent to tie her shoes. I jogged slowly in place to keep my legs loose.

It was a beautiful late September day in the midst of Indian summer. The red maples shone against the blue cloudless sky. Behind me the marble dome of the State House gleamed in the morning sun.

Leaves had begun to fall, and the red and gold mixed together for a vibrant collage all around me. I looked above the Providence Train station to College Hill. I could see the white spiral of the Baptist Church with dappled colors of the autumn foliage spreading upwards to Prospect Park.

I first began running in 1990. At that time the downtown CVS was just a 5K that was an afterthought someone dreamed up after a night on the town. It got little publicity. But at the time, I was in the throes of passion for the new sport I came to love. I ran it quickly and did not agonize over my timing or performance. My parents were both alive then. They came to cheer me on while my father took videos of all the runners at the starting line. I looked forward to running this race every year when summer turned to fall. I was proud to see it becoming a national event. Providence was a beautiful backdrop for an autumn race in the city I loved. It was inspiring to run along the winding streets bordered by the river. And everywhere the tall buildings provided a contrasting backdrop to the race route. The scenery had not changed much since then. But I had.

Slowly, we began jogging as the lady on the loudspeaker sang "God Bless America." I had to tread carefully to avoid the walkers in between the runners, all the time thinking of my breathing, my shins still sore from my Pilates class, and why did I have a bran muffin for breakfast? But with the city before me on a sparkling Sunday, I suddenly felt lucky. An unexpected surge of elation and joy ran through me. I had an instant flash of recollection of the many races of my lifetime and nostalgia swept over me. Thinking of years passed, I reflected on changes, opportunities missed, some taken, and the direction my life has taken me, as my feet pounded the pavement rounding the turn into South Main Street.

Mile one seemed endless. A small Asian girl whipped around me and nearly broke my stride. Across from me, a father and daughter struggled to keep together. I could hear a band playing ahead. The first water station left the road littered with slippery cups, and I finally spotted the mile marker ahead. A sweaty young boy next to me muttered about his knees, and I surged ahead. Another band around the next bend played an old Jim Morrison tune, and the firemen grinned in front of their gleaming red trucks. Someone cheered and clapped, and I could hear a train whistle in the distance. I tried to focus and visualize the pizza I planned to have after the race. But instead, I began to zone out. My mind wandered again to my early racing years.

The first race I ran was the Bonnie Belle in Boston. It was a 10K, which was the norm back then. Most races were 10K, and there was no walking allowed. There were also no strollers or pets. It was a race for women only, and it was a tough one with a few challenging hills that snaked around Boston Common. I remember taking the train from Providence, all excited in my new Nike running shorts. I met my sister at the starting line where she had driven in from Framingham. At first I ran slowly, at the end of the pack, near the ambulance. The fear of stopping and having to walk was very real. I had visions of riding the ambulance into the finish line. I remember puff-ing up one particularly steep hill near an underpass. All the women around me yelled and swore companionably while onlookers cheered us. I loved it. At that moment, I knew I could make it as long as I had the crowd and the support of all the other women who were struggling through the same issues. The camaraderie gave me the boost I needed to finish without even breaking my stride. My sister and I celebrated at the finish line. That was a runner's high I would never forget.

Suddenly mile two was near. I could feel the blisters begin-ning on my feet, but I vowed to ignore them. Now I became con-scious of my sweat, my heart pounding and the sun on my face, and my car keys jangling in my little pouch strapped on my wrist. My mouth was dry, and I envisioned a hot shower and cold beer as I rounded the corner to Memorial Boulevard. The crowd cheering us on grew larger. Several people stopped in their cars beyond the blockade to watch. One family had their three kids sitting on the roof of their car. I could smell the smoky remnants of last night's Water-fire. It reminded me of the smell of charcoal burning on a hot summer morning in Falmouth.

When I signed up to run the Falmouth road race, I knew I had hit the big time. It was over seven miles of hilly twisting roads in the middle of August. Running the route for the first time made me anxious and excited at the same time. The views were breathtak-ing. Mile one ended at Nobska light, a beautiful sight on a summer morning. The road twisted through woods for several miles and then suddenly the ocean appeared. The next couple of miles were hot, but the road paralleled the beach. Bands were playing everywhere. If I was lucky, I could catch a breeze, but sweat usually made it difficult to see clearly. During this hot stretch of the race, people usually dropped out. Families in shoreline houses along the way partied while we sweated. Hotdogs sizzled on grills. The next stretch was the hardest. Exhaustion and heat usually had taken its toll by that time. The marina and restaurants looked inviting, and it was difficult to keep focused. Finally, Falmouth Heights was straight ahead. I could see the giant flag waving, and I knew, as I flew down the steep hill to the finish line, that I made it.

I ran Falmouth eleven more times. It inspired me to run the Oak Bluff race every year along the beach in Martha's Vineyard and The Jingle Bell run in Newport. They were both beautiful races with challenging terrains. The sense of accomplishment I feel when I cross the finish line has given me all the confidence I ever needed in life. Many races I ran through the years were done in the rain, cold or blistering heat. But along the way, I always felt I was taking strides to accomplish much more than a race. Another hurdle achieved, another road successfully navigated.

The father and daughter were walking now. The Asian girl had stopped to tie her shoe, but I plodded on. I could see the new Westin Condos gleaming in the sunlight ahead and braced myself for the last hill. Picking up my pace, I gave it one last shot, as the cheering crowd passed by in a blur. I could see myself, in slow motion, hands held high, grinning with delight, as I flew over the finish line, running on empty.

An Attitude Adjustment

by Joni Pfeiffer-Moser

I don't think it ever stopped snowing in the winter of 2015. It certainly seemed that way! There had been bitter cold temperatures here in Rhode Island with much more snow than usual. Every day the forecast droned on: *another three inches on the way today, more tomorrow, the heavy wet stuff over the weekend.* My patience had worn paper thin. From my living room, I could see our sunless deck, which overflowed with gorgeous blooms in the summer, replaced by drifting snow which rose halfway up the window. We couldn't open our sliding door! I was acutely aware of what my body and my mind wanted to do in this unusually cold winter. If only I could curl up in a fetal position under the covers in my cozy, warm bed and hibernate until spring! Some animals have the right idea. I wished I were a bear! I'd had these thoughts before during snow-piled winters in Rhode Island, but I hadn't always experienced such a severe dislike of snow and winter. The decades have piled up since I was a winter-loving kid who delighted in skiing at Yawgoog, loved making snow people in front of our home in Rumford and later in Cumberland, loved sledding on the hills at Agawam Hunt and ice skating at Slater Park, loved teasing and throwing snowballs with my brothers and friends on our way to East Providence High School. But as time passed on and I got older, all that changed; snow and winter became frustrating inconveniences that got in my way and controlled my life! It is true that usually, there is less snow along the coastline where I live now in South County, but not that year— not in 2015. From Woonsocket to Westerly, the snow fell constantly, not only busting town and city budgets, but also creating happy children with a multitude of no-school announcements.

In spite of having grown to dislike winter, some truths needing attention also crept into my brain. I realized that at my advancing age, I positively do not want to waste any day in this one life of mine. *Live each day to the fullest*—that's my motto! But how was that possible when chronic cold and snowy winter weather controls my life each year for three or four months—what I do, how I feel and what I think about? To be honest, most of my family lives in Rhode Island, and my spouse and I cannot financially afford to go south to escape winter. That's our reality. The time had come for me to deal with this in a more positive way. I had tossed this thought around in my head previously, but actually achieving it, I did not know how to go about that. But as things happen, sometimes unexpectedly, I came across the seeds for a possible adjustment a couple of days after yet another huge snowstorm.

On one bleak January morning in that nasty winter of 2015, with a steamy cup of coffee in hand, I peered outside and saw the pleasant looking, middle-aged gentleman who had been hired to clear the snow-piled walkway in front of our condo from yet another unwelcomed storm. It was icy cold, and I could see he was working hard. Feeling pity for the poor guy, I poked my head out from behind the storm door and invited him to come inside to enjoy a break with a hot drink to which he consented. I led our conversation with the usual ain't-it-awfuls about the continuous mounds of snow and the frigid temperatures. I didn't have one positive thing to say. But my guest uttered a surprising, "Oh, I really love the winter," to which I thought: *what is he—nuts?*

I was jarred from my whining and groaning by his relaxed, reassuring manner, his smile, and clear, straightforward delivery. I thought, *Okay, I'll bite!*

"How come?"

"Well, winter is one of the four seasons, and I like 'em all. Over the years, I've lived in other parts of the country and even the world. I found while I was in certain tropical climates, I missed the change of seasons in Rhode Island where I grew up in Burrillville."

I probed further. "So you're saying that even though you've experienced a warmer climate consistently, you don't want it all the time?"

He nodded.

"But what could you possibly like about winter? It's so cold and miserable, and this year, it's even worse. It snows and snows and snows!"

"Oh, but I like snow!"

With scrunched up eyes and face, I sputtered. "Come on! You *like* snow?" This was not a child I was speaking with. I didn't recall knowing too many adults who *like* snow.

"Well, it can get to be a little much sometimes, but it provides a chance for winter sports especially skiing, which I absolutely love. Ah, there's nothing like it!"

"So you like winter sports. But the freezing cold, you like that," I jeered.

"No, but I dress warmly, you know, layers. And I love to be snug in a warm house. I love to sit in front of a crackling fire. I don't focus on the cold."

"Fires are nice, but don't you worry about slipping and falling or your car sliding off the road?"

He paused. "Well, nah, not really. I actually don't mind driving on snow-covered roads."

"Huh. And why is that?" I asked Mr. Snow Lover. *Is this guy for real?*

"Because it's quiet, it's peaceful. I like the challenge of driving on slippery roads. I know how to control most skids. It's kind of fun."

By now I'm wondering how two people could be so opposite! I decided to ask my cheerful guest about the change in seasons from a philosophical or spiritual perspective.

"My friend, tell me. How did you get to this point of loving all the seasons even the tough one winter? What kind of meaning does it have for you?"

His poignant answer: "I savor all four seasons' differences— the rebirth in spring, the full growth and maturity of summer, the winding down in fall and the stark beauty of winter."

Smugly, I blurted, "Yes, but in winter, everything dies!"

"No! Everything doesn't die! Some of it is hibernating, waiting to bloom again in spring!" There was that idea *hibernate* again!

I took a deep breath, "So, come on, tell me: is there anything you don't like about winter? There must be something!"

"Yeah, well, I don't like wet, salt-melted slush on the roads and the dirty water sprayed on my windshield. I'm not real happy the days are so short. I hate potholes!"

"Yup, Rhode Island is noted for potholes! But still, you like four seasons and you would not be as content with your life if there were no winter. Right?"

Like a serious preacher pontificating from his pulpit, he replied: "I think the four seasons reflect the stages in our lives. I like the changes. They make me happy and give me a lot to look forward to."

My winter-loving philosopher guest finished his warm drink and headed out to complete his shoveling task. He left me with a deep dose of sincere appreciation about winter to digest, a different point of view. I was not convinced I'd accomplish a complete turnaround, but he did get some of his ideas through to me. Instead of complaining, maybe I should consider the beauty of the ice glistening on branches, the crunching of the snow beneath my feet, the stillness after newly fallen snow, the stark beauty of a black and white Rhode Island landscape in the woods of Charlestown or Exeter, and going deeper, the seasons reflecting the stages of our lives. But I knew to change my perspective would take some work.

Coincidentally, the next morning on my Facebook page a recipe was posted for making ice cream with snow! My snow-loving friend hadn't mentioned that! But with my new hopeful desire to turn my attitude around, the next day I decided to try it! It was a beginning! Hope springs eternal!!!

Rogue Island

by Norman Desmarais

Rhode Island is sometimes referred to as Rogue Island. Some may attribute this to the moral fiber of our politicians but the designation may go back to the founding of the colony. The Pilgrims came to America in search of religious freedom but they did not grant it to their followers. They landed at Plymouth, Massachusetts in 1620 and founded Boston in 1630. They expelled Roger Williams for his dissenting beliefs in 1636 and banished Anne Hutchinson two years later.

Roger Williams purchased some land from the Narragansett Indians and founded the colony of Rhode Island. Anne Hutchinson also purchased some land from the Narragansetts for 10 winter coats and 20 garden hoes. She became the first woman to establish a town in America: Portsmouth, Rhode Island. The first settlers of the new colony, followers of Roger Williams and Anne Hutchinson, were no longer welcome in Massachusetts.

Rhode Island measures about 65 miles, north to south, and about 45 miles, east to west. Its irregular coastline, plus that of its 36 islands, give the colony a total of almost 400 miles of shoreline. This made it very difficult to patrol the colony when Parliament decided to enforce the Navigation Acts and to curtail smuggling. The colony became a haven for smugglers and pirates like Edward Hull, Thomas Tew, William Kidd, Captain John "Long Ben" Avery, Captain Thomas Paine and Captain Black Sam Bellamy who flourished in Rhode Island. They found it easy to evade British authorities and conceal their treasures in the many coves and caves in the rocky cliffs along the coast.

Two young women, walking near the cliffs of Newport after a storm in the summer of 1949, found a heavy iron chest which the storm uncovered. The women said the chest was about 20 inches long, 12 inches high and 12 inches wide. It was locked and it was too heavy for them to move, so the women abandoned their effort. Another storm delayed their return and, by the time they went back, the chest was gone.

Paper Money Controversy

The first appearances of the designation Rogue Island in print deal with the paper money controversy that dominated local politics between 1786 and 1791. This was the underlying issue for the state's repeated refusal to ratify the U.S. Constitution. The first occurrence of the designation was in the August 23, 1786 issue of the Pennsylvania Journal which gave an account of fraud and injustice in the repayment of a mortgage more than four years after its due date:

As fraud and injustice have, in the state of Rogue-Island, not only been encouraged, but even enjoined by solemn law: many, no doubt in this Commonwealth, would wish to be made acquainted with the progress some of its citizens make in these laudable sciences—we shall therefore occasionally communicate such instances as come to our knowledge—and, as a preface, we have extracted from a Providence paper of the 5th instant, the following,—"State of Rhode Island, &c. To all Whom it may concern, Know ye, that Samuel Bissel, of Exeter, on the 15th of July, at North-Kingston, lodged with me the sum of £. 22 5s and 4d lawful money, due to Pardon Tillinghast, of West Greenwich, in the county of Kent, yeoman, in full of the principel and interest of a certain mortgage deed, payable 20th of March, 1782; and that the said Samuel Bissel hath in all respects complied with the law respecting the paper currency and that the said Pardon Tillinghast has been duly notified thereof...1

John Trumbull and a group of staunch Federalists (David Humphreys, Joel Barlow and Lemuel Hopkins), known as the "Hartford Wits", wrote an epic poem called the Anarchiad. It was directed against the enemies of a firm central government, particularly Rhode Island, a bastion of antifederalism. It reads, in part:

> *Hail! realm of rogues, renown'd for fraud and guile,*
> *All hail! ye knav'ries of yon little isle.*

And ends:

> *The wiser race, the snares of law to shun,*
> *Like lot from Sodom, from Rhode Island run.2*

The following year, "A friend to mankind" accused the state legislature of villainy when it accepted paper money as legal tender instead of gold and silver:

Villainy established by Legislature Authority in the State of Rogue-Island.

> When now the mob, in lucky hour,
> Had got their enemies in their power;
> For in the ferment of the stream,
> The dregs have work'd up to the brim,
> And the rule of topsey turveys,
> The scum stands swelling on the surface.

To what a miserable situation are we reduced? In how despicable a light are we viewed by foreign nations?— Are there no bounds prescribed for villainy?—Or, are the basest of mankind ever to prey on the industry and frugality of the honest few?—

I have long been a silent spectator of a game which must, in a short time, inevitably end in our ruin;—but, sensible to my inability to remedy the evil, by giving advice to a set of people pre-determined against the voice of reason, to this moment I have remained quiet.

The late Assembly still persisted in their determination of forcing their favourite coin down the throats of those who are not willing to receive it in payment for property, when the value is not equal to more than an eighth. —— Strange infatuation!—and how much more incredible, when the very men who have ever argued and voted for such an unjust measure actually discharged their tavern expences, at the close of their last session, at Little Rest [Kingston, RI], at the rate of eight for one!

To investigate the causes why a paper currency in our present situation, must bring certain ruin on this state, is a task which, was I equal to, I am not disposed to engage in. It is sufficient to say that the dire effects it has already occasioned are so evident, that the blind themselves may almost see.

The husbandman finds no sale for his produce; the mechanic, the labourer, have no encouragement:, no employment; a general stupor prevails; a total lethargy has overwhelmed the state; and commerce, the only support of a flourishing country, has taken to herself wings, and flown away.—He alone thrives, who has heretofore received a value from his neighbor which the present lawful and unjust privilege of returning, as an equivalent, a few sorry rag bills, intrinsically not worth a farthing.

I will state a simple question or two and let Justice determine their property.— Suppose (for we can suppose nothing too enormous for a legislature to countenance, after their refusal to grant the request of his Excellency Governor Bowdoin, and, by their neutrality, granted protection to those bloodhounds, rebels and runaways, from our friends in the state of Massachusetts) if the late Right Honorable Assembly had granted full liberty for high-way robbery, with those men, for the justification of whose conduct the authority of the state is now pleaded, be praiseworthy in turning out and supporting the robbers? Or, should they enact, that the elder branch of a family might destroy the minor, to enjoy in a greater degree the estate of their ancestors; or, like the Britons at the time of Julius Caesar's invasion, oblige parents to murder their child, should he unfortunately be born with a cloven foot, would this* wolf in sheep-skin approve such villainy?

You, my countrymen are led to believe, that this favourite paper could be kept at the standard of specie, would the merchants give it a currency.—This is a most palpable falsehood, served up by those cunning knaves, is the most plausible of their reasons for continuing it a tender.

No! believe me, my countrymen, the instigators of this diabolical plot never wished to preserve it from depreciation. Their grand and sole object would then have been marred, and just debts could not have been paid off at an eighth of their value.

Shall the same laws which would deprive a poor culprit of his life, for passing a dollar reduced one half by alloy as a real one, countenance a perjured villain in defrauding an orphan, a widow, his friend, his brother, and perhaps his parent, of seven eighths of their whole property? Is it just? Can there be any plea in favor of such unparalleled wickedness? That there is a great and good God, let these fiends of hell remember, and shudder at the fate which awaits them. To plead an error of judgment hereafter, will be but a shallow subterfuge for daring so impiously to insult the laws of the benevolent Ruler of the universe.

A friend to mankind.

Providence, 29th March, 1787 3
* A writer in favour of the present measures.

When the University of Rhode Island conferred an honorary doctorate on Daniel Shays for his stand against controversial debt collection and tax policies in Massachusetts, some of Shays's opponents had this to say:

> New-York, June 5
> The University of Rogue-Island, have, it is said, lately conferred the honor of L.L.D. (Doctor of Musket, Swivel, and Cannon Law) upon his Excellency Major General Shays and that a diploma, upon parchment, will be forwarded to the general as soon as the governor can acquire HARD MONEY (by loan, or otherwise) sufficient to pay the postage to Vermont.4

The accounts in the New-Hampshire Spy and the Massachusetts Gazette go on to say:

> A letter from Vermont mentions, that general Shays grievously complained of having been very greatly plundered during his late peregrinations | and that too, as he supposes by some pretended friends and well wishers to his intended reform of government; for that he had, in a small portable wooden box, six hundred and seventy-two ducats in gold, 1329 guilders, and some stivers in silver; all of which, together with the box itself, and some of his most important letters (of foreign and domestick correspondence) were taken from under his bed in the night between the 24th and 25th ultimo! That he hath not been able to get any the least intelligence of the vile robbers that took them away; but that from some circumstances, he apprehends the money hath, before this time, found its way into the treasury of Rogue's-Island. The gold, he says, was tied up in a leather bag, and marked PETER THE GREAT in capitals.

> The general proposes to issue a proclamation offering a large reward for either the recovery of the money or apprehending the scoundrels who robbed him.5

Rhode Island was the last of the thirteen colonies to ratify the Constitution. Most of Rhode Island's Federalists abstained from voting in the March 1788 referendum and the state refused the Constitution by a margin of 11 to 1. Some towns rejected it unanimously: Coventry (180 to 0), Foster (177 to 0), Scituate (156 to 0) and Cranston (101 to 0). The state's repeated refusal to accept the Constitution was based on opposition to the Country Party's paper-money platform.

Lansingburgh, Nov. 20.

Extract of a letter from a fellow in Newport (Rogue-Island) to a gentleman in this town.

"We have nothing new this way but the new Constitution— it will not go down here—nine tenths of the people are against it—. IN MY opinion it is a damn'd impudent composition and an insult on the understanding and liberty of the KNOW YE's."

Extract of a letter from a gentleman in Providence to his friend in Albany.

"It is with pleasure I inform you, that all honest men in Rhode Island (who, alas are not very numerous) are anxious for the adoption of the new Constitution, knowing it to be the only thing that can extricate us from the present distress and prevent future slavery."6

An opponent of the Rhode Island Great-Bridge Lottery made the following proposal:

An adventurer in the Rhode Island Great-Bridge Lottery, proposes to the gentlemen who so handsomely manage it, alteration of its title—and would recommend the name of Rogue Island, or, if they please, North-Mill lottery, secundus.7

Christopher Cudgelled, Esq. was probably a state legislator who was assaulted by one of his opponents for his vote on a particular piece of legislation. Newspapers reported his slow recovery:

The Honorable Christopher Cudgelled, Esq. is very slowly recovering from his wounds.

Perhaps some tender law of the moral state of Rogue Island might be applied by way of emollient and cataplasm to scarified honor.8

A sexagenarian recalled that Newport was once a bigger, more thriving city than New York and was the envy of New Yorkers:

I do not believe that a more restless, eager, excitable multitude be found on the face of the globe than that which congregates daily in Wall Street, (New York.) What a contrast does a scene here present to the good old times of the Knickerbockers, when Newport was a bigger place than New York, and when it was the hope of the burghers that the city of Manhattan would yet rival her more flourishing sister of Rogue's Island! But now, forsooth, the real Dutch blood is almost exterminated; and it is enough to raise from last sleep the steady old pipe smokers, the bustle and rattle that are going on above their graves.

I found my way, a week or two since, into Wall street, just before the hour of exchange—the first time for a twelvemonth. A Southern friend was with me, returning home from

Saratoga. Crowds were collected about the sidewalks, little knots hurrying down to the wharves; man stopped man inquisitively, and parted with a mutual shrug of the shoulders. Something was evidently in the wind.

"Ah," said I to my companion, as we passed the lower corner of the Exchange; "here comes my old friend D——; man and boy, he has haunted Wall street this hundred years, more or less; and, if there's any mischief afloat, he knows all about it."

He was passing me with a firm, rapid step, his eyes bent on something or somebody beyond. "Hale and hearty yet!" I exclaimed, "though I have grown quite too old for you to remember. Time was, sir, when I was your junior, but it has gone faster with me than with some folks. What's the deuse to pay in Wall street?"

"Ah Mr. L— ," replied the old gentleman in specs, for it was none other, "the report is the British Queen is in possession of the revenue cutter."

"What's the matter?"

"Ah, that's more than I know. The story I tell as it is told to me, and I do not vouch for the truth of it. There are a thousand rumors, but I am going to find out the facts."

As fond of facts as ever, D——? I cannot comprehend how you can still take such an active interest in affairs. For my part, I have got out of them these ten years. I believe you were born in Wall street, and your ghost will haunt it a century after you are gone. But I see you are in haste; good morning."

The active gentleman waved his cane courteously, and was off in a twinkle. My companion looked askingly. "That, sir,"

I replied, "is the biographer of Burr, and is more than suspected of being the Spy in Washington. He has been a parti-
san for half a century, and has never asked for office at the
hands of the Government or the People."

"And why so?"

"Simply because he would never be bothered with it. He
would never consent to merge his individual influence and
character in an office. He prefers his independence, and will
have his own way in spite of the world."

Thus conversing, we threaded our way through the crowd to
the park in front of the Courier and Enquirer.

"Let us take a look at the bulletin."

"Not a word of the British Queen! We will inquire at the door.

"What's the matter? what's the matter?" They were all askers
and listeners.

"I understand," said a rosy-visaged, plump gentleman, that
there are two cutters alongside of her; but what they want is
more than anybody can tell."

"Where is the consignee? What says he about it?"

"I have just come from the consignee's, and he is just as wise
as you are," says Tompkins

"The Government has given orders to search every steam-
vessel that goes abroad, for fear that there may be some more
elopements of sub-treasurers," suggests Smith.

"The truth is, gentlemen," said a dapper young man, who had just come up the street, fresh from the scene of action, "the marshal has gone aboard to inquire after an absconding creditor."

Higgins looked on in contempt. Higgins knew. Higgins knows everything. Higgins shrugged his shoulders, and observed that the "fact" was that there was some specie on board not entered at the custom-house, and that, consequently, the custom-house had determined to detain the Queen.

Still the fever increased. What could be the matter? Specie smuggled, sub-treasurers giving leg bail, creditors absconding—what was the truth? Still grew the wonder. An hour elapsed; despatches had been received from the British Minister. The British Consul was about taking up his connexions. Important news from Canada had just come in, and the Queen was to be kept back four and twenty hours. All creation was hurrying down to the wharves.

For two whole hours Wall street was in a ferment. The brokers forgot their second board, and stocks were described as in a fluctuating condition—to continue so until this mystery was solved. Cotton trembled. Flour looked blue. Indigo turned pale. United States Bank shivered. The only articles that rose in the market were hemp and eggs.
At length the Queen was again seen gliding majestically through the water—and as she passed the noble floating palace, the pride of our gallant navy, a hearty cheer bade her God speed upon her ocean path!

The knots of eager loungers and lingerers were broken up. Wall street went home restless and unsatisfied. Money dealers passed sleepless nights. Old Grimes determined to sell out all his stocks the next day; nobody could tell what would happen next. Bluenose was horror-struck, and ascribed the whole matter to the rapid progress of Democracy, which was ruining the country; and Varmount thought it quite time to shut up shop, if foreigners were to be permitted to cut such capers with impunity.

With an impatient hand did many a worthy citizen open the papers of the next morning, to learn some authentic account of this mysterious occurrence. I must plead guilty to no little anxiety myself. I wished to know what it was that had unsettled markets, knocked down our stocks, and created such a whirl and whiz of excitement on our metropolitan exchange.

The mystery was solved in a single word. It was nothing connected with our northeastern boundary, or Canadian insurrections. Mr. Fox, though he had been all the summer at Washington, had no hand in it. Mr. Buchanan was guiltless. There were no decamping sub-treasurers. There were no revenue cutters, but an oyster boat and a Whitehall barge. There was no man in the claret-colored coat!

"What then could it be?" exclaimed my wife, from an impulse of curiosity in females not indecorous or unusual.

"Why, my dear," said I, laying down the paper and replacing my specs, "the steward had forgot the eggs." ——N.Y. Mirror9

In the years after the Civil War, the question of the currency again came to the fore. In the following discussion of "greenbacks" states (Sixth), Rhode Island was called Rogue's Island because it struggled longest to retain specie as the currency.

A Few Precepts Respecting "Greenbacks."
To the Editors of the Evening Post:

It was a wise as well as a witty man who said in 1863 that greenbacks were like the Jews: the issue of Abraham waiting for a Redeemer. If the Ohio Democrats got their way it was a prophecy more full of woe than any Jeremiah ever uttered.

It is humiliating to be obliged to explain the alphabet to grown-up people, but it seems to be necessary on this currency question; and editors of newspapers can do it more effectively than other men because they can print in conspicuous places short and pithy reductions ad absurdum, which, like the "silent comforters" of the pious, are certain to be read and possibly taken to heart. For instance, the daily quotation of the value of greenbacks in your money article is of great service. Nothing has more befogged the mind of the unthinking public than the usual quotation of gold at a premium. The vulgar notion is that more is paid for gold, not less for greenbacks, and that there is an actual loss of property in exchanging government paper for gold.

Keep before the people the stale truths:

First, that gold is a commodity like wheat, iron or cotton—a commodity that all men the world over, longed for, and have longed for since history began and which they are willing to accept in exchange for whatever they are willing to part with.

Second, that the government stamp on a gold coin merely indicates officially the quantity and quality of the bit of gold stamped for the sake of convenience.

Third, that any man, anywhere, would, if necessary, cheerfully accept in exchange for his goods gold in ingots or lumps, if satisfied of its fineness and weight; but nothing but force would induce him to take paper, even green paper that

105

has not on it a promise to pay gold which he believed would be kept.

Fourth, that gold is capital, intrinsically wealth, as well as currency; but the paper is not capital or wealth—it only represents it; and if the representation proved false the paper is worthless.

Fifth, that all the greenbacks in the United States, if the promise to pay them in gold is proclaimed to be false, will become worthless, except to light a fire or to furnish pulp for a paper mill.

Sixth, that if the inflationist Democrats establish the principle of no promise on the greenback, and no payment in specie, and a greenback be merely a bit of paper with the peculiar quality of discharging debt, the greenback will not long retain this attribute beyond the time when existing debts are wiped out; no one will take it who is not obliged to, and soon no one will offer it to respect himself. After the Revolutionary war the Legal Tender act remained in force, but it was considered as disgraceful to offer paper as to plead usury; the state of Rhode Island, which struggled longest to retain it, was called Rogue's Island in consequence.

Seventh, that where values are unsettled by legislation or otherwise, capital refuses to embark in any enterprise; it seeks only snug and safe places, hides itself, goes abroad if necessary, but cannot be obtained for paper; consequently the inflationists by their success must defeat every object they pretend to have and exalt one, which they pretend to detest—repudiation—and this would be of no advantage.

The interest on our debt, large as it is, is not felt by a prosperous country, whereas a fluctuating currency is the greatest and most ruinous tax that can be laid. You might also explain why greenbacks were so successful a stimulant during the war. They were then notes issued for value received by a government that wanted everything. A new issue would be accommodation paper, which prudent business men hesitate to touch, even when put out by firms in good credit. Real money cannot be made out of nothing, no matter what that nothing may be "based on," any more than force can be created by an engineer. You can transmute force—you cannot create it. It is a physical impossibility.

Pardon me for those hints. No doubt they have often occurred to you. But this currency question is so serious that no reasonable man can keep quiet. We fought for years to keep the nation whole and to give four millions of blacks their rights. Of what use was that sacrifice if the nation is to be a nation of fools and knaves, and twenty millions of whites are to be despoiled of their property!

J. W Newport, R. I. October, 1875.10

The currency issue was resolved with the Currency Act of 1900 which made the gold dollar the monetary standard and set its value at 25.8 grains of nine-tenths fine gold. The act also set up a gold reserve of $150,000,000. The gold standard lasted until 1933.

Notes

1. August 12. *Pennsylvania Journal.* 2094. August 23, 1786 (p. 3).

2. The poem begins in *American Antiquities. The New Haven Gazette* and *Connecticut Magazine.* October 26, 1786 pp. 287-288 and continues in 12 subsequent issues through September 13, 1787. See particularly the December 28, 1786 issue p. 353 where this excerpt appears. See also Conley, Patrick T. *Rhode Island in Rhetoric and Reflection: Public Addresses and Essays.* East Providence: Rhode Island Publications Society, 2002. p. 87ss.

Norman Desmarais

3. Villainy Established by Legislature Authority in the State of Rogue-Island. *The New-York Morning Post* And *Daily Advertiser.* 972. April 28, 1787 p.2.

4. *Pennsylvania Journal.* 2173 June 13, 1787 p. 2. *New-York State,* New-York, June 9. *New-Hampshire Spy.* II: 68 June 16, 1787 p. 271. New-York, June 9. *Massachusetts Gazette.* VI: 339 June 15, 1787 p. 3.

5. *New-York State,* New-York, June 9. *New-Hampshire Spy.* II: 68 June 16, 1787 p. 271.

6. *The New-York Morning Post* and *Daily Advertiser.* 1158. December 1, 1787 p.2. Lansing-burgh, Nov. 20. Extract of a letter from a fellow in Newport (Rogue-Island) to a gentleman in this town. *American Mercury.* IV: 178. December 3, 1787 p. 3.

7. *The Norwich Packet.* XX: 991. March 14, 1793 p.3. *Western Star.* IV: 18. March 26, 1793 p.3.

8. *Boston Gazette.* 13:52. February 28, 1803 p. 2. *The Connecticut Centinel.* XXX: 1513. March 15, 1803 p.3. *The Visitor* (New Haven, Connecticut). I: 19 March 8, 1803 p.149.

9. What's in the Wind! by a Sexagenarian. *Alexandria Gazette.* October

10. *Evening Post.* 74. October 8, 1875 p.1.

Freedom Rings Through Public Art

by Paul F. Caranci

R hode Island is arguably the place where American freedom was born! Long before the first acts of aggression sparked the American Revolution, Roger Williams and John Clarke promoted the concept of religious liberty to a tyrant king an ocean away. But what is freedom? Ask ten different people and you might just get ten different explanations of what it is. One dictionary defines it as a philosophy; the power to exercise choice and make decisions without constraint from within or without; autonomy; self-determination. While the definition itself may be elusive to some, a concept that is universally recognized is that freedom isn't free. It is provided to us at an enormous cost and with great personal sacrifice. Perhaps even less obvious than the definition are hundreds of visual illustrations of freedom on display all around us in the form of public art.

For generations people the world over have memorialized the sacrifices made at the altar of freedom in sculpture, statuary, monuments and memorials. They honor the war dead, their acts of valor and martyrdom, their everlasting gift to those who remain beneficiary of their lionheartedness. Rhode Island is no exception to this phenomenon and perhaps nowhere in the Ocean State is there a more vivid and diverse collection of these monuments-to-freedom than in its capital city of Providence.

The very concept of freedom, however, conjures images of the bonds and shackles that deny some form of liberty to people of the world. We live in a country that is free, and generations have fought wars to ensure their children, grandchildren and others maintain that privilege. Some seek the freedom that this great nation provides by fleeing the figurative bonds of their own country of origin.

109

Still others seek freedom from the eternal flame that may await them in death. Regardless of the freedom sought, the desperate attempts to gain it are frozen in public art for all to study and enjoy.

That enjoyment, however, is predicated by the need to actually see and recognize the sculpture, statuary, monuments and memorials that constitute public art. How is it even possible to miss something the size of these tributes? After all, these monuments-to-freedom are prominently featured in open spaces where thousands of people, perhaps tens of thousands, pass each day. They are designed to attract public attention. They are installed to great fanfare and public ceremony. Yet, as Richard Jarden, former Assistant Professor of Sculpture at Rhode Island School of Design, once wrote, "Public sculpture is very difficult to see. On an immediate level what is going on around it, behind it and sometimes on it can be as engaging as, or often more engaging than, the sculpture itself. We pass by sculptures every day without noticing them because they are mute, frozen helplessly in time, while we have the ability to move, even to move away." Jarden's prescient statement is as true today as it was when the ink of his pen was pressed to paper some 37 years ago, perhaps even more so with the complexity of life in the 21st century. So let's take a moment to look at some of the monuments-to-freedom, those artistic masterpieces that hide right in our plain sight.

Religious Freedom

English born Roger Williams might best be described in modern terms as a maverick. In criticizing the canon of New England Puritanism and attacking the theological foundations of Quakerism, Williams was banished a heretic and fled the Colony of Massachusetts in the winter of 1635 under threat of imprisonment, deportation and possible death. He and a small band of followers crossed the colony's southern border at the Seekonk River and entered the freedom of a heretofore unknown territory, there to establish the colony of Rhode Island and Providence Plantations. Freedom from the fear of Puritan revenge, however, was not enough to quench Williams' thirst for autonomy. And so, from the perch of this new society, Williams enlisted the assistance of John Clarke to draft a Charter framing a colony government devoted to protecting individual liberty of conscience. Risking death, they petitioned a tyrant English King, Charles II, to approve the Charter that according to historian, Dr. Stanley Lemons, marked "the first time in modern history that a monarch signed a charter guaranteeing that individuals within a society were free to practice the religion of their choice without any interference from the government." This lively experiment, as it has come to be known, is perhaps Williams' most endearing legacy.

Providence has two public statues dedicated to the founder of religious freedom. The first rests in Roger Williams Park and was dedicated on October 16, 1877. The 7½-foot-tall-standing bronze statue is set upon the top of a 27-foot-tall granite monument framed with a base of five steps that ascend to the shaft from every direction. A 6-foot-high bronze female figure representing Clio, the Muse of History, is set into the pedestal figuratively entering Williams' name into antiquity.

The second statue of Williams sits in Prospect Park overlooking the city that he founded. This 1939 tribute is made of Westerly granite and stands 14 ½ feet tall. The statue is set between two granite pylons that form a rectangular arch projecting slightly from the terrace. The figure of Williams is shown to be blessing the city as he stands at the bow of his canoe. Beneath the monument's base lie the mortal remains of Rhode Island's champion of liberty. Originally buried on his own land under an apple tree on Benefit Street in 1684, Williams' remains were exhumed in the nineteenth century and placed in the tomb of descendant Stephen Randall in the North Burial Ground until being placed in a bronze container and relocated to his final place of rest under the base of this colossal monument.

Many other representations of Roger Williams, founder of religious freedom, can be found in Providence, throughout Rhode Island and spread across the nation.

Freedom From the Shackles of Slavery

Men, women and children have been enslaved since biblical times, but in the United States of America, slavery has become largely synonymous with mistreatment of African Americans. Between 1709 and 1807, merchants of Rhode Island supported at least 934 slave voyages to the African coast and transported an estimated 106,544 slaves to the New World. Trading rum for slaves was a lucrative business and ships sailed from Newport, Bristol and Providence.

Here, John Brown and his brother played a commanding role in the triangle trade of rum, slaves and molasses, and they often used their slave-trade-induced wealth to support philanthropic causes. The Brown family's contributions to Rhode Island College, for example, were so great that the name was changed to Brown University. On that East Side campus, several of the early buildings were constructed utilizing the labor of slaves. It is fitting, therefore, that the sole monument acknowledging Rhode Island's early dependence on the slave trade, and celebrating the freedom of emancipation, lies on that campus.

The work of contemporary sculptor Martin Puryear is actually comprised of three distinct elements. The first is a partially submerged giant ball and chain with the third link of the chain broken, symbolizing the end of slavery and celebrating the freedom of all men guaranteed by the Constitution. The second element is a cylindrical plaque inscribed with information acknowledging Brown University's connection to the eighteenth century trans-Atlantic slave trade and located near the ball and chain. The third element is the brainchild of Jo-Ann Conklin and the Brown Public Art Committee and is the actual site itself, as this memorial is located near University Hall, an 1870 campus building constructed with the labor of at least three slaves.

Emancipation – Let Freedom Ring

No celebration of freedom would be complete without a statue of the Great Emancipator. It was the Nation's 16th president after all that risked his office, the cohesiveness of our country, indeed his own life, for the cause of freedom. Monuments, statues and memorials in his likeness and to his virtues appear in virtually every state in the Country.

In Providence, the statue of Abraham Lincoln stands at the eastern entrance of Roger Williams Park on the Miller Avenue traffic island. Constructed in the early 1950s by local sculptor Gilbert Franklin, the statue was funded with a 1922 bequest from Mr. and Mrs. Henry W. Harvey, prominent Providence jewelry manufacturers.

Franklin's life-size bronze statue of Lincoln is mounted on a ten-ton granite base and depicts the President in classic pose. His arms rest at his side, and he is wearing traditional period clothing. Lincoln's right hand clasps a piece of paper thought to be his notes from the Gettysburg Address. According to the keynote speaker, Roy P. Basler, American historian and Lincoln expert to the Library of Congress who addressed a large crowd at the statue's dedication ceremony, "the sculptor captured the President just after giving the Gettysburg Address." During his speech, Basler cited Lincoln's tolerance perhaps "as a counterpoint to the spirit of McCarthyism" that pervaded a number of years of that decade.

Lincoln's courage ended the scourge of slavery that plagued this country since its founding and granted freedom to African slaves throughout the land. While the true intent of Lincoln's largess was not immediately apparent to some, his actions set the stage for the equality so desperately desired by the framers of our Constitution and allowed freedom to finally ring throughout these United States.

Freedom Personified

There may be no single object in Rhode Island more symbolic of the freedom that we enjoy than the Independent Man perched atop the State House dome. Despite being the State's most recognizable symbol of liberty, his "birth" was little more than a substitution for a statue of a different iconic Rhode Islander.

It was January 8, 1895, and members of the Rhode Island Historical Society discussed the newly announced plan to build a single, permanent State House to replace the five current State Houses scattered throughout Rhode Island. Members adopted a resolution expressing their unanimous view that a statue of Roger Williams should surmount the dome of the capital building about to be constructed. The Roger Williams Society concurred, and the testimony of those groups was presented at a meeting of the Board of State House Commissioners a few days later. Also presented was a suggestion by State House architects that an 11-foot bronze of a modestly dressed woman called "Hope" might best represent the State's 200-year-old motto with dignity. After listening to the testimony and discussing the options, the Commissioners voted to allow a Massachusetts resident and Rhode Island School of Design professor, George T. Brewster, to design the statue giving Charles McKim, the project's lead architect, final approval.

In the end, it was Brewster's design of an 11-foot muscular man clad only in a loin cloth that was mounted on the State House dome some 235 feet above street level. Weighing in at 500 pounds, the figure's right arm is outstretched and in his right hand is a 14-foot spear. His left hand rests upon an anchor, the State's symbol. Brewster called his creation "the Independent Man" because it epitomized the independent spirit of Roger Williams. The Commission agreed that the Independent Man was the essence of all things Rhode Island.

In 1927 the statue was the victim of a serious lightning strike that caused a significant amount of damage. Repairs were made in place, but 42 copper-plated staples were required to patch him up. Then on August 9, 1975, in preparation for the celebration of the 200th anniversary of the Nation's birth, the Independent Man was taken down from his perch for refurbishment marking the first time in over 75 years that nothing topped the 4th largest unsupported marble dome in the world.

Freedom once again reigns over all Rhode Island with the Independent Man firmly back in place atop the State House dome, and everyone who gazes up at the magnificent display can be heartened by the symbol of freedom and independence that he represents.

Freedom from Famine

It is not only Americans that crave freedom but people the world over. During the years between 1845 and 1851, the British Colony of Ireland experienced a terrible famine, one that was having a devastating effect on the colonists. With two-fifths of the Irish population dependent on the cheap crop for survival, the disease and starvation resulting from the so-called "Great Hunger" was responsible for the death of over one million people and the emigration of as many as one million more. In just six years, the British Colony lost between 20 and 25 per cent of its population. During the worst year of the famine, more than 250,000 desperate people departed the ports of Ireland in an attempt to make a better life for themselves and their families. Many chose to do so in America hoping to benefit from all that freedom has to offer.

But not all citizens of the United States were waiting at the docks with open arms. Much like the feeling toward some of today's immigrants, the Irish were met with hostility, bigotry, hatred, prejudice and signs in business windows intoning "No Irish Need Apply." As with most immigrant groups, the Irish were accepted over time, and today monuments to the Great Famine and exodus dot the landscapes of many great American cities.

Providence is no exception! On November 17, 2007, a great monument was dedicated along the Providence River Walk not only as a powerful acknowledgement of the sufferings of those impacted by the Great Famine, but also as a lasting tribute to the triumphs of those who overcame the adversity. Sculptor Robert Shure crafted a multi-component memorial that unites the despair of the past with an enduring sense of optimism for their lives in a new land. The monument consists of "three larger-than-life statues of Irish figures mounted on a stone base. A mournful woman cradles the limp body of a relative whose life was ended far too early at the hands of hunger and disease. They face toward the life left behind, while walking in the opposite direction, is a third figure in full stride symbolizing the start of a new life in the land of plenty.

A walkway leads from the statue to a commemorative wall on which is inscribed the history of the famine amid the Irish immigration. The sidewalk below the wall illustrates a map of the coasts of Ireland and America and emphasizes the "audacious journey of the Irish people to the United States" in their quest for freedom.

Freedom from the Clutches of Hell

Perhaps one the most intense depictions of freedom in public art graces the campus of the Rhode Island School of Design. For here on the Frazier Terrace, a small two-tiered green area located off Benefit Street, is sculptor Gilbert Franklin's work called Orpheus Ascending.

The three figures atop a spreading pond frond that rises out of a fountain basin portray the mythical Orpheus attempting to rescue his lover Eurydice from the grasp of hell. Greek myth gives us the story of the gifted musician Orpheus, a man who could charm anyone with his music. Upon discovering that his wife Eurydice had succumbed to the bite of a snake, the grief-stricken Orpheus descends to the depths of hell to attempt to soften the hearts of Hades and Persephone with his music. His talent is successful in overcoming death, as the devil allows Eurydice to return with her husband to earth with the proviso that Orpheus walk in front of her and not look back until they both reach the upper world. As he re-enters the land of the living, Orpheus forgets his vow and turns to look at his wife who has not yet reached earth. She immediately vanishes from his sight, forever cast back into Hades.

The moving myth demonstrates just how important freedom from the fires of hell was to the ancient Greeks. That urgency remains ingrained in the hearts and minds of all men even today.

Fighting for Freedom
The Civil War

The bloodiest war in American history is also the one to which the greatest number of statues are associated. Pitting brother against brother might be considered the epitome of evil, but it was a very common feature of a Civil War that separated families as much by geography as ideology. So common are the statues commemorating this war and the people who fought it that two appear at opposite ends of Kennedy Plaza in Downtown Providence. While not the most aesthetically pleasing of the two, the equestrian of Major General Ambrose Burnside is certainly the most controversial.

Dedicated in 1887, this Henry O. Avery design depicts one of the least productive Civil War Generals atop his horse and mounted on a granite base measuring 28 feet in height. The bronze statue, however, is far more impressive than Burnside's war record.

Though born in Liberty, Indiana, Burnside was fiercely loyal to William Sprague, the Governor of Burnside's adopted state of Rhode Island, and was quick to answer Sprague's call for a leader of the First Rhode Island Volunteers. But it's possible that the West

Point graduate's star rose too quickly. His early efforts earned him the notice of Abraham Lincoln who regarded Burnside highly. When Lincoln sought to replace General George McClellan as commander of the Army of the Potomac, he turned to Burnside who reluctantly accepted the President's appointment. At first he performed admirably claiming victory in North Carolina and achieving other Union triumphs in the early stages of the war. His star faded quickly, however, as he was handed responsibility for an embarrassing defeat at Fredericksburg, the most lopsided of all Civil War battles. Union casualties numbered 13,000, more than triple the number of Confederate losses. Two months hence, Burnside was removed from his command. He resigned his commission on April 15, 1865, following a second major gaff during the siege of Petersburg that, like the defeat at Fredericksburg, also resulted in a great number of Union casualties.

Despite his ineptitude on the battlefield, Burnside remained fiercely popular in Rhode Island where he won election to three consecutive terms as Governor and two in the United States Senate. Burnside died suddenly at his home in Bristol at the age of 57 while still serving in his second term in the United States Senate.

Thousands turned out for the 1887 dedication of his monument and many dignitaries, including keynote speaker General William T. Sherman, attended the ceremony. Rhode Island Historical Society President Horatio Rogers, who served under Sherman's command remarked, "His career is ended, his statue is done. Ambrose E. Burnside has passed into history. Rhode Island has spared naught that could attest her appreciation. In life she conferred her highest honors and dignities upon him; in death she has fashioned his form and feature in bronze, graven his name in granite, and reared them aloft in enduring testimony of her gratitude, and as an example of emulation."

In retrospect, General Burnside may best be remembered not for his military acumen, but rather for the Sideburn—the facial hair named for him. Despite his military shortcomings, it cannot be denied that he gave his all for the cause of liberty, proving yet again that freedom is never free, but the struggle to achieve it or retain it is always worth the effort regardless of cost.

Monuments to the Freedom Provided Through All Wars

It is not only the sacrifice of the Civil War that is recognized in public art. All major military engagements fought by American citizens in the fight for freedom are memorialized in such a way. Three of the major wars in which American citizens struggled for liberty are displayed in Memorial Park, also known as War Veterans Park located just west of the Licht Judicial Center on South Main Street.

The World War I Monument is one of the tallest of all the City's monuments. From this structure's 150-feet-tall perch, the heroic figure of Peace keeps watch over the Providence River and its city surroundings as a reminder of the war fought to end all wars. The fluted granite column was dedicated in 1929 as a memorial to the Rhode Island soldiers who defended our freedom in the First World War. Steps at the base of the monument lead to the shaft from all directions, and the first step is decorated with bronze panels depicting ships, planes and other implements of war. On the plinth itself are four large faces separated with an insignia of each branch of the military and inscribed with words from the dedication ceremony and with quotes from Abraham Lincoln, Woodrow Wilson and Ralph Waldo Emerson. A memorial frieze circles the column and represents the virtues of the Rhode Islanders that gave their all in the war effort. Above the frieze are listed the names of the war's major battles.

The World War II monument, located to the south of the memorial to the First World War, was dedicated in 2007. It is comprised of a 16-foot-circular colonnade with eight round granite 14-foot-tall columns supporting a 4-foot-wide granite cap and cornice bringing the total height of the monument to 18 feet. The granite floor beneath the monument's cap depicts a Mercator map with numbers referencing the war's major battles, the names of which are inscribed on the inside face of the eight column bases. In addition to the colonnade, there are two granite pylon walls each containing the names of the 2,560 Rhode Islanders who gave their last full measure for freedom's sake. Four contemplation benches stationed in front of the honor roll provide a place for visitors to view the names of the state's war dead. Each bench is inscribed with one of the four freedoms: freedom of speech and expression, freedom of worship, freedom from want and freedom from fear. Completing this monument is a granite stone imbedded on the monument floor that reads, "This monument is dedicated to the men and women of Rhode Island who served and those who died in the struggle to establish a world founded upon the four freedoms cited by Franklin D. Roosevelt in his address to Congress on January 6, 1941."

The final conflict memorialized in War Veterans Park is the Korean War Memorial. This 1998 addition depicts a single bronze soldier kneeling with his bowed head covered by a hood to stave off the bitter cold and frigid wind. He clutches his rifle in his hands keeping it at the ready. The statue conveys the soldier's deep sense of loyalty to his country, but also the loneliness of being forgotten, bringing to mind the war's nickname of "the Forgotten War" because few understood the impact of the war and fewer cared. This memorial pays tribute to the 39,000 Rhode Islanders who served their country during that conflict and was "designed to represent the spirit of service, the willingness of sacrifice, and the dedication to the cause of freedom that characterized all of the participants."

In addition to the artwork memorializing the aforementioned conflicts, the struggle for freedom in other entanglements is also cast in the bronze, stone and granite of public art throughout the City of Providence. These efforts include the American Revolution, the Vietnam War, the Spanish-American War and the Wars of the Middle East.

All Creatures Big and Small Desire Freedom

The struggle to be free can sometimes unite both man and beast. One of the most endearing stories of the intersection of the lives of people and animals is forever remembered in the simple bronze cast of a large Mastiff. Though the most widely photographed statue in all of Rhode Island, few actually know why The Sentinel occupies such a prominent place in Roger Williams Park.

While Thomas Frederick Hoppin honed his artistic skills as a young painter growing up on Westminster Street in Providence, Anna Jenkins, granddaughter of Moses Brown and one of the richest women in America, was about to face tragedy. While her family slept on a cold, otherwise quiet night in November 1849, a fire broke out in their home and quickly engulfed it. Black Prince, the family dog sleeping in the yard awoke, broke free of its chain, and barked loudly as it raced toward the house. The barking awakened 17-year-old Anna and her 15-year-old brother Moses, the only two survivors from the inferno on 357 Benefit Street.

Sometime after the fire, Anna and Hoppin met, were married, and built a new home on the site of the fire-ravaged mansion that caused so much pain to Anna and her family. Though primarily a painter, Frederick felt compelled to memorialize in sculpture the animal responsible for saving his wife's life so many years before. The 300-pound, life-sized bronze of the life-altering animal was one of the first of its kind in Rhode Island and such a striking example that when shown at Crystal Palace in London, won the gold medal from the New York Academy of Design. The bronze Mastiff wears a studded collar and has a broken chain draped over its back. It stood as a lawn ornament in the Hoppin's yard until 1896 when family members donated it to the City of Providence. It has since occupied several places at Roger Williams Park and currently greets visitors to the Park's world-class Zoo. Over the course of generations, it has become the Park's unofficial mascot with many visitors stopping to take a picture of their children sitting atop the large dog's back. Few of the unsuspecting photographers have any idea that the dog and its actions signified freedom in so many ways. In breaking free of its chains, Black Prince enabled the two children to free themselves from the flames that claimed the lives of all the others, allowing two people to meet, marry and forever memorialize the love of a dog for its family.

The expansive, yet distinct nature and breadth of the monuments, memorials, statuary and sculptures that dot the American landscape tell stories and evoke emotion. These monuments, like the stories themselves, demonstrate the various meanings of freedom. Specifically, those examples of public art invoked here, though diverse, are with singular purpose. Collectively, they are distinctive in detail yet compelling in nature, but each memorializes and pays tribute to freedom and those who gave everything to provide it.

Yes, if you ask ten people to define freedom you may indeed get ten different answers. However, while few can define it, most will agree that they know it when they see it and that they crave it. The public art in and around the City of Providence, the State of Rhode Island, and the entire world, provide us with the visual. It is up to us to see it. Richard Jarden indeed seemed prescient when he wrote of public art, "We pass by sculptures every day without noticing them because they are mute, frozen helplessly in time, while we have the ability to move, even to move away." Now however, when you do notice the public art that pervades our daily lives, you may better understand, and more fully appreciate the significance of the struggle for freedom that each represents.

Sisters of Bay Crest

by Kathy Clark

I creak. And when the Rhode Island skies light up, shadows cast upon my horsehair plaster walls can be downright scary. Water pelts against my delicate panes—ping, ping! When the wind gusts, one can feel the breeze created. Is it to suggest that I have escaped condemnation? Perhaps! I have weathered the likes of the Great New England Hurricane of '38 to the Blizzard of '78 and everything else Mother Nature could and would throw at me before and after these years. I stood tall during The Great Depression and even endured a war or two. Oak treads carry many to my crest where their eyes may witness a New England sunset or a blanket of haze suspended over my seaside community. My quaint rooms bring tranquility to guest. Pillows that lay upon my rope beds bring comfort to each weary head that rests there. And if one lies still in their bed during the twilight hours, they may hear a distant fog horn as their eyelids grow heavy. No, I am not haunted. I was born in the 1800s. Of course, I creak.

Since the 1600's, Newport, Rhode Island, has been adored by many daily and weekly visitors. For some, it has been a place to call home. You can walk the streets of Historic Hill and come across the survivors of the neighborhood: Touro Synagogue (the oldest in America); Redwood Library (the oldest lending library in America); and Touro Park (dubbed Pigeon Park by the locals), which embraces the Old Stone Mill (believed to have been built by Norsemen). Just a stone's throw away is the renowned and elaborate Viking Hotel where many of its guests can often be found relaxing in Touro Park sipping their morning coffee, walking their canines or reading the morning paper.

Newport has also been graced with high-society families like the Vanderbilts and their summer home, The Breakers, which is presently owned by the Preservation Society of Newport County, and Jacqueline Kennedy's (First Lady and wife of President John F. Kennedy) childhood home, Hammersmith Farm. Breathtaking views of the Ocean Drive's Atlantic shoreline and beautiful coastal mansions will lay easy on your eyes. Later on through the years, Rhode Island's prominent seaport hosts the crowd-pleasing Jazz Festival (b. 1954) and the Folk Festival (b. 1959). But clustered amongst these long-admired institutions, you will find Italianate-type architecture. Easy to recognize, these buildings are best known for their ornate porches, windows, and hip roofs. These towering clapboard homes will make you sigh when looking up to their three-story frames. Who were the people who owned them? Allow me to introduce one such family.

When Scottish immigrants, John and Betsy Brims, came to Newport, little did they know that someday their brood of daughters (five in all) would independently own some of these homes that many today hold in awe when curious eyes peer through their camera lens. The daughters were Elizabeth Brims born 1884 in Scotland; Catherine Brims born 1888 in Scotland;Mary Brims (Molly) born 1891 in Newport, Rhode Island; Ethel Brims born 1893 in Newport; and Emma Brims born 1895 in Newport.

Unlike their older, married siblings, unattached Molly and Ethel sought their own homes out and about Historic Hill. Their previously owned homes can be found to this day on Catherine Street, Old Beach Road, Kay Boulevard, and Brooks Avenue. They operated these homes as rooming houses or guest houses for many years until the Great Depression touched each one. Because the fallen economy had claimed many properties and age claimed their youth (thirty was old back then), 38- year-old Molly and 36- year-old Ethel sold their individual homes, pooled their finances and purchased one home on Corne Street, Bay Crest, which helped alleviate financial burdens during that dark time. Although a purchase of this magnitude was unheard of for women and being unmarried and child

-free by choice, a rarity in the 1920s, the two compact women purchased the home in 1929 from Carol and Joseph Hall. Their strong Scottish heritage of working hard and depending on one's self to survive was inbred in them. Even though this home was a privately-owned residence, the thick tufted duo thought that with three floors and nine bedrooms, they believed it should be a guest house like their former domiciles. With that said, Bay Crest Guest House was brought to life.

Unbeknownst to Molly and Ethel, the two learned that their newly purchased home housed some sort of vapor-bath establishment in the mid-1800's. A physician by the name of Charles Peckham lived there alone and ran it as a Turkish bath, or as many had referred to it as a vapor bath, which aided patients with their rheumatic troubles. There is no proof that the baths ever took place there except for a framed newspaper ad displayed on one bedroom wall stating it was so.

In 1931, after ambitious youngest sister Emma, 36, had her fill of flying solo, she joined her older sisters and helped run the guest house. In 1959, Molly died at 68 leaving Ethel and Emma to shoulder the responsibilities that came with their sisterly venture. The two retained Bay Crest as a guest house until their well-established time here on earth dictated that it was time to quit the guest house business in the late 1970's. By the 1990's, the historic property would be signed over to their niece Lottie Keith and then passed on to Lottie's five children to keep as the family's summer residence. Ethel Brims lived until 1991 and the last surviving sister, Emma, celebrated her 96th birthday in November 1991, just a few months before her death.

Signatures of a time passed can be found in the brown-bound guest book that sits on a black marble table in the main foyer. Yellow and worn from time, you can thumb through the pages and find many New Yorkers who came to visit, including actress Lee Remick back in 1954; New York's Casino Theater owner Sari Stanim in

1962; an array of newlywed couples in the 1940s; and numerous naval officer candidates throughout the years.

Although the house remained a quiet refuge to its visitors, the house did not come without negatives. In 1948 there was a stove fire on the second floor and a break-in around 1969. And the continuous upkeep of painting, wallpapering and cleaning alone would exhaust anyone let alone these petite women. Some jobs were done by them, and some were hired out when they got on in age.

As record states, Bay Crest was built in 1837 by builder Seth C. Bradford and purchased by its first resident, Benjamin Stevens, that said year. From there, there had been four previous owners before the Brims sisters became the house's long-term dwellers.

Sitting on one of the two front porches with family historian, Don Keith, the great nephew of the sisters of Bay Crest, we sipped our Dunkin' Donuts coffee and gazed out at the surrounding houses and passersby. Every once in a while a hand waved our way or an utterance, "How are you?" followed. I thanked him for telling me about the road his aunts took to owning such a wonderful heirloom and for his knowledge of something that took place years before he was around. Then he said, "The most important thing to remember in life is that you should be aware of your surroundings. A person should always know where they came from, where they're going and what is in front of them. Knowing is what keeps us who we are. It keeps us solid. Knowledge is everything." The historian added, "This house stands three stories high, high on Historic Hill, and my aunts made it what it is today." He showed me the wooden Bay Crest sign and said, "About the 1960's, it fell into disrepair but will soon be restored and will hang from this porch once again." Then he offered, "Because you can see the bay from the crest of this house, the name Bay Crest was probably coined for that reason. Everyone names their house in seaside communities. It's just something that we do."

As my curiosity grew, I had to ask if he thought that the house was haunted. He chuckled, "It is a fact that when a neighbor slams their car door, it does sound like someone's coming up the stairs. If you understand where the noises are coming from, then there's nothing to fear. Sounds resonate through the frail windows. That's all it is. That's being aware of your surroundings."

For a better view of the old house, he walked me across the street where three large hydrangea bushes are nestled against the clapboard structure. As our interview came to an end, Keith continued, "See those bushes? No matter who comes and goes, one thing is for certain—those three hydrangea bushes have seen it all. They were planted by my Aunt Ethel when my mother, Lottie, was a child of 10, maybe 11. I remember them when I was a kid, and I'm 60. And my mother, she's 87."

An Island, A Revolution and Heavy Scythes

by Bruce Wilcox

I would like to introduce you to my family. My ancestors have been in Rhode Island since early 1633. My father's paternal side of the family, settled on Aquidneck Island. On my mother's paternal side, my ancestors have been here since 1661. Ancestor's on my mother's maternal side landed in Rhode Island in 1645.

For hundreds of years, the only known inhabitants on the small island off the coast of Rhode Island were Manisses Indians. The first known exploration was conducted by the navigator Verrazzano, an Italian explorer in the service of the king of France. He was credited for discovering the island around 1524. It wasn't until 1614 when a Dutch explorer named Adrian Block arrived, that the island became known as Block Island. Adrian Block was a Dutch trader and was the first European to visit the island. Twenty-two years after Block landed on the island, a trader from Boston by the name of John Oldham and his crew came to Block Island to trade with the Manisses Indians. The Manisses were part of the Narraganset Indian Tribe. The Indians killed Oldham and his entire crew. Most New Englander's learned of Block Island after hearing the tragic news of the slaughter of Captain Oldham.

My direct maternal descendants arrived at what is now the town of New Shoreham, Rhode Island. The Dodge family established by my patriarch Tristram Dodge, arrived on Block Island in 1661. This was on my mother's maternal side. Tristram Dodge was one of the first 11 settlers of Block Island. He came by way of Newfoundland to teach people fishing and navigate the waters off Block Island.

Many Dodge members were fisherman and farmed the land of Block Island. Several were quite qualified marine pilots. They operated ships from the mainland to Block Island and across the globe and back. Dodge family descendants brought visitors and goods from the mainland to Block Island. At the time of the early 1900's, this journey was treacherous. There were many shoals and rocky areas that had to be navigated during tidal changes. Tad Dodge was one of the best pilots there was. Tad began piloting in 1879, and by 1926 he had been piloting for 47 years. His father Joshua Dodge was the first one to receive his Rhode Island pilots license. At that time, of the 27 pilots from Rhode Island, 8 were from Block Island, and 6 of those were named Dodge. Pilots were paid by the depth of the water a ship drew. All ship navigation during this time was done prior to the invention of radar, which was not until 1935. Captain William Talbot Dodge, "Tal" as he was known to friends and family, led ships to safe harbor for 71 years. Tad and his wife also ran a successful bed & breakfast (a term we know today) but at the time, Tal listed his profession as "Boatman" in the Rhode Island Census of 1880. Tal Dodge's parents were Joshua & Lucretia Dodge, and his wife was Phoebe Ray Ball.

Joshua and family owned a ship named Independence, and Joshua piloted ships in Narragansett Bay for 56 years. The Independence was an oil burner and went under the business name of Block Island Pilot Service. The owners were Captain William T. Dodge, William E. Dodge, and Joshua T. Dodge.

During the time of prohibition, there were many ships transporting liquor and goods for clients. On April 15, 1922 in New York harbor, Captain Tal Dodge and his first mate were arrested and detained to check barrels of whiskey, against the manifest for the locked shipment. The vessel was the W. Talbot Dodge, a 49 & 1/2-foot schooner. Dodge pilots were transporting goods all over the world. It was not fully legal to transport liquor until 1933. One of the most reported trips in the Block Island Times in May 1930 was the following:

During a dark, foggy night, Captain Tal Dodge (on his 70th Birthday) successfully transported a ship loaded with 6000 tons of coal into Providence harbor.

Descendants on my maternal grandmother's side of the family had a tremendous impact on the foundation of the Industrial revolution. My 8th great-grandfather (Joseph Jenckes II) founded the city of Pawtucket and formed the basis for industrial tools, and textile operations. His father (Joseph Jenks Sr.) was the first to develop the process of taking "bog ore" and using the cast metal process to create tools and parts that were part of the industrial revolution in America. The Saugus Iron Works was the first site to have scythes formed and designed by Joseph Jenckes. A cast pot, known to be one of the first articles cast in North America, is now held in a vault at the Peabody Essex Museum in Salem, Massachusetts. Joseph Jenks Sr. was the first to build a forge in Lynn, Massachusetts. Joseph Jenks, emigrated to the U.S. in 1643. Joseph Sr. was issued a patent to manufacture scythes and tools. The site was in Saugus, Massachusetts. These scythes remained essentially unchanged in shape for 300 years after the design created by Mr. Jenks.

The story of Pawtucket, Rhode Island. began in Colebrook, Buckinghamshire, England, in 1599, when Joseph Jenks Sr. was born. His son Joseph Jenks Jr. was born in 1628 in Colebrook, Devon England. Joseph Jenks II arrived in the U.S.A. in 1645. Joseph Jenks II intended to settle in Warwick, but discovered the abundance of lumber, bog ore and superior river power on the Pawtucket Falls side of the river. The area where the forge was established was near the Seekonk River. Joseph Jenks II is credited with forming the city of Pawtucket, Rhode Island.

On the Paul side of my family, (my mother's maternal descendants), the family was comprised of farmer's, machinist's, and technologists. Relatives originated in Wakefield, New Hampshire. Hiram Paul (a mason) built an 800-foot-long stone canal in Wakefield, New Hampshire. The site is now on the register of historical landmarks and is called the "Newichawannock Canal"

Aunt Henrietta Paul was a D.A.R. (Daughters of the American Revolution) member. The patriot that she was supporting played a large part in the Revolutionary War.

Joseph Jenckes also fought in the Revolutionary War.
Two other paternal descendants fought in the Civil War. Both were captured at the Battle of Monroe. John Tunnicliffe, and his son-in-law, Edmund Congdon both died in the Andersonville Prison Camp. One died of starvation and disease. The other died following amputation of his leg due to infection caused by a bullet wound. Andersonville was the most horrible and worst of the Civil War Camps.

The most interesting thing about all of this family history and genealogy is that previous to 1990 to 1992 I had almost no knowledge of these ancestors. Then something tremendous happened. A close aunt began performing research and genealogy on our family. What she learned was both astounding and eye opening. I was always the story teller of the family. I would be the scribe. I would write down events, record family picnics, and relate these stories year after year, reflecting on the stories and colorful family members. Because I expressed an interest in this history my Aunt Marilyn shared all of her research and findings when she completed research. To this day I still retain the original legal sized manila envelope she presented to me. I cannot tell you how many times I have used the material within that envelope. At the time my copy was given to me by Aunt Marilyn, all of the data was contained on paper records. PC based tools genealogy were early and cumbersome. As computerized tools for genealogy improved and changed, data had to be translated and in many cases re-typed into newer genealogical software tools.

In the timeframe from 2005 to 2008, I invested in the one of the latest genealogy software database programs available. I began to enter all of the data from the paper records. Over the course of more than two years, I was able to complete the entry of the research. There were some discrepancies of BDM (Birth, Death, and Marriage) records. I checked the verification of entries where my aunt had a notation in column. Some of these dates could be verified by cross-referencing other records and U.S. Census Records. Hours upon hours were invested, searching for the "truth" about records. Because of my background in engineering, research, and technical databases, I was hooked. Many nights I could not put the database away, or come away from the computer. I would manage to get some sleep, but then awake early to continue searching for the correct date and completing the verification.

I am proud to be part of a family that heavily influenced the Industrial Revolution. Our country would not have produced tools, textiles, & scythes had it not been for the entrepreneurial contributions of Joseph Jenckes Sr.

I look forward to continuing my research and genealogical study. Currently on my maternal side, we have documented 47 generations back to 355 A.D.

I would like to finish by citing: "Prior to the Industrial Revolution, which began in Britain in the late 1700's, manufacturing was often done in people's homes, using hand tools or basic machines. Industrialization marked a shift to powered, special-purpose machinery, factories and mass production." www.history.com/topics/industrial-revolution.

Agriculture in Rhode Island

by Al Bettencourt

Let's face it, Rhode Island is not an agricultural state and it never will be. But in the last decade, especially since the great recession in 2008, RI Agriculture has been a bright spot in Rhode Island's economy. The number of farms in RI has actually increased in the past decade as has the amount of land dedicated to farming. According to the 2012 Census of Agriculture, the number of farms in RI increased from 1,219 to 1,243 with the amount of land dedicated to agriculture increasing from 67,819 acres to 69,589 acres. There was even a more dramatic increase from the 2002 Census of Agriculture to the 2007 Census of Agriculture. In 2002 there were 858 farms on 61,223 acres up to 1,219 on 67,819 acres in 2007 for an increase in farms of 42% and increase in land in farms of 11%. A farm is defined by the United States Department of Agriculture (USDA) as any place where an agricultural commodity worth more than $1,000 was raised.

For many years there was a decline in farms in RI. Over 100 years ago, according to the 1910 Census of Agriculture, there were 5,292 farms in RI on 443,308 acres. While the number of farms and land in farms has fluctuated over the years there was a steady decline in the number of farms and land in farms up to 1992. In 1992 there were 649 farms in RI on 49,601 acres. (The paragraph above will tell you how farms there are now.) Granted, the biggest increase in farms has been on small farms with a range of 1-9 acres. The number of small farms increased from 208 in 2002 to 433 in 2012. The number of farms with sales less than $2,500 per farm increased from 287 farms to 451 farms while the number of sales of greater than

$100,000 per farm stayed about the same from 112 to 108 farms from 2002 to 2012.

Why has the number of farms increased? The "Buy Local" movement has had a lot to do with the recent increase in the number of farms. But during the 1980's, the RI Farm Bureau working together with Governor Garrahy established a commission to study the decline of agriculture and what could be done to reverse the trend. They came up with several recommendations that became law. The new laws were, the Right to Farm Law, Ag-land Preservation Commission and the Farm, Forest and Open Space (FFOS) program.

Under the Right to Farm law, farmers cannot be stopped from carrying out normal farming practices. Farms often give off bad odors and make noise. Neighbors cannot stop normal farming practices under this law.

The Ag-land Preservation Commission buys the development rights from farmers for their farmland. Farmers use the funds they get from this purchase to continue to run the farm. As of 2015 over 100 farms have sold their development rights. Farmers retain full rights to use the farm but are not allowed to develop it into house lots or businesses (other than maybe a farm stand). Funds for this program are usually a partnership between the federal and state government and a local land trust or similar entity. The development rights are usually retained by the local commission. The federal and state governments get their funds from tax dollars. On the state level, each election year there is usually a referendum question asking tax payers for funds for open space. This question is usually one of the most popular questions on the ballot and is always passed by a wide margin.

Under the FFOS program, farmers have their land appraised at the farmland value rather than the highest and best use value. This significantly reduces the amount of property tax they have to pay. However, they must agree to keep the land in farming for at least 10 years. If they develop the land within the 10 year period they must pay the city or town back the amount of money they saved.

In recent years the State has finally started listening to the RI Farm Bureau on the inheritance tax issue. When a son or daughter inherits the farm it is appraised at it full market value, which is usually house lots. In order to pay the inheritance tax it is often necessary to sell at least part of the farm as house lots. RI Farm Bureau kept telling the General Assembly that if they kept appraising farmland as house lots, they would become house lots. In 2012 the General Assembly finally passed a bill that would allow inherited farmland to be appraised as farmland. This act allowed the average size farm (around 50 acres) to be inherited tax free.

As stated above, the "Buy Local" movement has had considerable influence on the farm industry in RI. This article started by saying RI is not and will never be considered an agricultural state. According to the RI Division of Agriculture RI farmers only raise 1% of the food consumed in the state. In a document entitled "A Vision for RI Agriculture, Five Year Strategic Plan" (which can be found on line) it is stated that the Ag Industry probably generates over $60 million in production. It also states that for each dollar generated in the Ag Industry another dollar is generated in the non-ag sector. This is in reference to so called "value added" products such as making jam from grapes and pickles from vegetables. So the ag industry probably generates well over $100 million in the state's economy. If you include landscaping, the so called "green industry" generates over $354 million according to the study mentioned above. Again when you think of RI you probably don't think it would ever be in the top 10 of some part of the agricultural sector of the nation. But you would be wrong! According to the 2007 Census of Agriculture, RI led the nation in direct sales as a percent of farm income.

Another area in agriculture where RI is number one in the nation is farmland value. According to USDA Land Values Summary (August 2015) farm real estate is worth $13,800 per acre in Rhode Island which is the highest land value in the United States followed by New Jersey at $13,000 per acre. The average cost of farmland in the USA is $3,020 an acre. It is as low as $510 an acre in New Mexico. This is a double edged sword for RI farmers. It helps current farmers get real estate loans to run their farms. But because land in RI is so valuable, new young farmers can't afford to buy it. The Division of Agriculture in RI is working on a program to make land more affordable for beginning farmers. It should be available in 2017.

Direct sales are the key to the success of RI Farmers. According to the RI Division of Agriculture (DAG) there are 38 farmer's markets "registered" with DAG. That is up from a handful in the 1990s. There are several markets not listed on the DAG web site, so the number of markets is probably closer to 50. There are other methods of direct market sales other than the farmer's markets. Obviously there are the traditional farm stands such as Confreda's and Schartner's (the largest stands in RI). But there are several organizations that also facilitate direct sales.

The most popular organization is Rhody Fresh. Seven local dairy farmers have banded together to form the RI Dairy Cooperative whose nickname and brand name is Rhody Fresh. Rather than selling their milk to a wholesaler (the largest milk dairy cooperative in the area is Agri-Mark, which makes Cabot Cheese), they have their milk processed by a dairy in Connecticut (Guida's) and sell it directly to grocery stores in RI, nearby Massachusetts and Connecticut. They started out in small markets because the small markets did not charge a slotting fee to sell their milk. Stop & Shop and Shaws were going to charge a slotting fee and Rhody Fresh could not really afford it when they first started. But so many customers asked for Rhody Fresh milk that Stop & Shop and Shaws asked the farmers to put their milk in their stores with no slotting fee. Rhody Fresh now sells cheese and butter as well as milk and half and half and has been in business for over 10 years. (A little known fact; for a brief period the RI Dairy Cooperative was known as the Proud Cow. That is the name they were going to call the milk until they hired a professional PR firm that came up with Rhody Fresh and the logo of the Holstein cow with the RI map).

Another promotion program not as well known as Rhody Fresh is Rhody Warm. This is the nickname and brand name of the RI Sheep Cooperative. They make blankets from locally grown sheep and sell them directly to the public. They asked Rhody Fresh if it was okay for them to call their blankets Rhody Warm, and Rhody Fresh cheerfully agreed. Each year a unique pattern is chosen for the blanket and is named for one of the lost villages that are so much a part of Rhode Island history (Last year it was called Ram Tail Mill collection and the year before it was the Nooseneck Village collection). In early June an average of 2000 pounds of wool is collected from members and the process begins. There are close to fifty sheep farmers in RI. Look up Rhody Warm on line.

Founded by RI farmers in 2005, the RI Raised Livestock Association (RIRLA) is a member-based, member-driven organization. All Board members are working farmers. Assisted by grants from the RI Foundation and the US Department of Agriculture, and with support from the RI Rural Development Council, the RI Raised Livestock Association is now an established and growing non-profit partially supported by its Processing Scheduling Service (PSS). Besides the PSS, RIRLA now offers many additional benefits to its members including trainings, networking and other educational events for farmers, technical assistance, grain discounts, a quarterly newsletter and more. According to the 2012 Census of Agriculture there are over 300 farms in RI that raise animals for meat.

The largest farm organization in RI is the RI Farm Bureau which was established in 1954. The Rhode Island Farm Bureau is an independent, non-governmental, voluntary organization of farm and ranch families united for the purpose of analyzing their problems and formulating action to achieve advancement and, thereby, to promote the national well-being. Farm Bureau is local, county, state, national, and international in its scope and influence and is non-partisan, non-sectarian and non-secret in character. Farm Bureau is the voice of agricultural producers at all levels. You don't have to be a farmer to join the RI Farm Bureau. You can become an Associate Member for a small fee.

The next largest farm organization in RI is the RI Nurserymen and Landscape Association. Nursery is the largest agricultural industry in RI based on value of crops sold. The Rhode Island Nursery and Landscape Association is rooted in a long tradition of horticulture. In 1919, the Rhode Island Nurserymen's Association (RINA) was formed by a small group of Rhode Island retail and wholesale nurserymen. The Rhode Island horticultural industry is made up of multi-generation family businesses whose hard work helped to showcase Rhode Island growers as some of the world's preeminent propagators and growers of trees and shrubs. As the organization grew in the early 1960s, the RINA board of directors expanded the membership to include the landscape industry and sod farms that were switching out of potato production. (Hence the new name, RI Nurserymen and Landscapers Association, RINLA).

The RI Food Policy Council is a self-appointed organization. The Rhode Island Food Policy Council's work is coordinated by a statewide collaboration of diverse, committed and engaged stakeholders from all sectors of the food system. The Rhode Island Food Policy Council creates partnerships, develops policies, and advocates for improvements to the local food system to increase and expand its capacity, viability and sustainability.

The purpose of the Ag Partnership was to create a five year strategic plan for agriculture for the state and to implement that plan. It consists of several import agricultural organizations and the RI Division of Agriculture. The plan was completed several years ago and the committee is now working on implementation. The plan can be found on line.

Only a few of the agricultural associations in RI are mentioned above. There are over 30 farm organizations that belong to the RI Ag Council which is just about one of the oldest farm associations in RI (established in 1924 by law). Their membership includes the RI Forest Conservators, RI Fruit Growers Association, Future

Farmers of America, Little Rhody Poultry Fanciers, RI Dahlia Association, RI Ayrshire Club, RINLA, RI Farm Bureau and on and on. They meet three times per year and discuss local farm issues. Almost all of these organizations can be found on line.

There are several movements in RI (and the nation for that matter) to try to help promote local food. The Farm to Table movement has seen a lot of restaurants offer local food. The Farm to School program is now run by Farm Fresh RI and its goal is to get local food into the schools. From small beginnings as a Brown University student thesis back in 2004, Farm Fresh RI has grown into an impactful non-profit organization implementing programs that enhance the food system of our region—with particular attention to low-income access to fresh food and farm viability. One of the ways they support local farms is through market-building programs (retail, wholesale, processing) that engage and connect tens of thousands of eaters with thousands of RI, MA, and CT farmers. An example of their impact, in 2015 alone, their Market Mobile transparent wholesale distribution system moved $2,248,898.97 on behalf of small farms and producers in RI, MA, and CT. And that's not counting the other market opportunities other programs create, from institutional buying to farmers markets throughout the state.

In addition to all the private programs and institutions mentioned above the state and federal government also offers aide to local farmers. The United States Department of Agriculture (USDA) plays quite a role in the promotion of agriculture in RI such as programs through the Farmer Service Agency (FSA). With 51 state offices and 2,124 county offices, including offices in U.S. territories, FSA implements farm programs and farm loans to farmers and ranchers across the country. To help administer these programs and services are FSA County Committees, which replaced the New Deal AAA Committees in the 1950s. Each year, approximately 2,500 county committee members are elected by their peers to help administer farm programs and services.

The Natural Resources Conservation Service (NRCS) is a USDA federal agency that works hand-in-hand with the people of Rhode Island to improve and protect their soil, water and other natural resources. For decades, private landowners have voluntarily worked with NRCS specialists to prevent erosion, improve water quality and promote sustainable agriculture. NRCS employs soil conservationists, soil scientists, agronomists, biologists, engineers, geologists and resource planners. These experts help landowners develop conservation plans, create and restore wetlands, restore and manage other natural ecosystems as well as advise on storm water remediation, nutrient and animal waste management and watershed planning.

USDA also has a presence in inspecting meat plants in RI.

The RI Division of Agriculture promotes agriculture in the state and administers certain programs to help farmers such as the Purchase of Development Rights, administration of pesticide licenses and pesticide distribution, enforcement of the Right to Farm Law and the Farm, Forest and Open Space program. The Division also administers the GAP program which is Good Agricultural Practices. Farmers must take a course in good agricultural practices and agree to an annual "audit" of their practices such as testing water and keeping food clean.

Cooperative Extension is part of the University of Rhode Island and provides an Agricultural Agent who offers farmers advice on plant nutrition soil management. Other scientists and specialists at URI also offer advice to farmers.

RI Farmers do have wide variety of services available to them, but there are services that are lacking. It is almost impossible to have a tractor fixed in the state of Rhode Island and there are only a few places to buy a farm tractor and parts for a tractor. It is very difficult to buy agricultural chemicals such as fertilizer and pesticides in the state at wholesale prices.

Thus although it has a small presence, there is a significant agricultural industry in the state of Rhode Island. With the demand for local food increasing more and more, the RI Agricultural Industry is likely to continue to grow. Goals from Food Solutions New England are that by the year 2060 New England farmers and food producers (such a fishermen) will be able to provide 50% of the food needed for the New England population (check Food Solutions on line). You can help achieve these goals by observing the state agricultural motto: Get Fresh Buy Local!

Most of the facts and figures in this article were found in the US Census of Agriculture published by the United States Department of Agriculture. Information about various farm organizations was obtained from their web sites.

A Brave Knight
A Tribute to a Rhode Island Landmark

by Leo C. Frisk, Jr.

O nce upon a time there was a knight in day clothing. He stood as tall as a short person possibly could, and he smiled with a frown as he told of his journey. Here is the tale of how this tall, short, thin, fat, man, boy's adventure took place.

He drove himself to his fate in the faraway towns in the nearby city. He roamed far and wide through the narrows on his trusted steed, a horse that could not pass the farthest weed. A nearsighted beast with its master aboard sailed through the desert. The trees were so tall, the sun so cold, and the days so dark, he traveled at night.

He feared nothing, but everything frightened him. He was a hero, a man, a true coward at heart, but this did not stop him as he traveled onward through this dangerous city-side town.

Up one hill and down another, these plains were hard to ride in. These flatlands never moved. It must have been the horse—its gallant knight riding high above, keeping watch for danger, as he looked behind him while they went forward on. With his head turned to the side, he could never know where they had been or where they were going, but he would at least know where they were not going to be.

Backward they traveled, then forward, again. Forward through time that trusted steed and he, onward into their greatest adventure of all.

It began on a hot winter's night. The sun wasn't shining, but the moon sure was bright. The air was hot and filled with the odor of air, and the smell was enough to fill up the nostrils, which was a good thing, because there were no gas stations nearby, and the trusted steed needed all of the fuel it could burn. Backward they went, one step at a time forward. Those stairs sure were hard to climb.

It had been a long and tedious journey, crossing that road, the road of life. Through all of the good times and all of the bad times, and Charles Dickens, and everything, too. But he, the gallant knight, had made it to where the chicken had forever been—across the road.

The jungle had long since disappeared, and the plains, hills, and valleys had all been crossed. It was time to complete the beginning of this journey that had started so long ago today.

The stairs built a stairway to heaven as they wound up toward the sky. The brave knight looked down as he climbed, or I should say, as his trusted steed climbed. All he did was sit in an upward position on top of it. They went down the spiral stairway, climbing and climbing their way toward heaven. The shortsighted horse with the long-range vision and the brave knight upon galloped on, taking one step at a time. This was going to be a long journey, so the knight had packed a lunch—two carrots and a ham sandwich for the horse.

They had been traveling for a long time, ten minutes, when the brave knight realized he had lost his water. This did not discourage the brave knight because he knew there was water there. There was water somewhere, near.

He reached down and grabbed. He had to hold on tight because the horse ran like it was walking on the moon. There was water. The canteen had fallen between the horse's legs, and when he grabbed it, the horse ran like it was going up a mountain down a hill. Faster and faster, up the down stairs they went, or did they? Bubbly, bubblery, bumpity bump!

It appeared as if they were running on a piano keyboard—clickity clack, clackity click, lickity split! Oh, look at that! White is white, black is black, take the ring then give it back.

Up and down, round and round, down and up the brave knight went. It was as if someone was playing music. There was music in his head. There was music in the air. There was music everywhere. Around and around the brave knight went. Up and down again, and again. What was this mysterious place? It had taken so long, such a short time to get here. The journey had taken miles of feet, hundreds of minutes, and thousands of seconds, and the food was gone and the water had bubbled out and oh, oh, his trusted steed would not stop running, and the stairs seemed like they were always there.

Then out of nowhere, the music stopped. The trusted steed stopped. The journey had come to an end. The brave knight had won, and his victory song would be heard by the deaf for centuries of days to come. He jumped from his trusted steed and ran as fast as he would need. He walked as fast as he could run right over the cotton candy machine and ordered a big one, an extra-large snack to fill up his belly for the journey back home across the road where this little boy lived and played in the fields and woods and especially in his imagination.

Johnny's ride on the merry-go-round had finished, and so has his story about a place called Rocky Point.

A decade-old amusement park stood for years alongside the greatest clam-cake-and-chowder hall in all of Rhode Island. It had been visited by nearly every resident of this state at one time or another enjoying its majesty. However, several years ago it was torn down and soon is to be replaced with—well, no one is sure for now. A once proud landmark whose roller coaster rides, its magical carousel and Ferris wheel, which kissed the Rhode Island skyline, now a vacant lot, sits silent with only the motion of the tides to keep it company.

Leo C. Frisk, Jr.

The greatest tribute we can all pay to this once-proud land-mark is for us who had the privilege to have gone to Rocky Point to pass those memories down to those who will never be able to enjoy the chowder, clam cakes and our day at the Park.

Under the Thirteenth Star

by Mark Perry

Being under the thirteenth star indicates that Rhode Island was the last of the original thirteen colonies to join the union. Last, yes... but certainly not least because there are many firsts for which Rhode Island is known, dating as far back to the Revolutionary War and the Industrial Revolution.

In a state where the current population is primarily Catholic, it is notable that the First Baptist Church in America originates in Providence. Sitting at the foot of college hill, this downtown church was founded by Roger Williams in 1638. The church was built to accommodate several thousand people, but on its first Sunday service, only the first five rows of pews were filled. Rhode Island's population, however, was rising at a rapid rate during that time, and it was a sign that Williams had confidence in Providence's future. Williams was a visionary and founded Rhode Island with the importance of separation between church and state, providing religious freedom for all, a part of the state's history that many Rhode Islanders are still proud of today. This religious freedom could also indicate why a little more than a century later in 1763, America's first Jewish Synagogue was founded in Newport. Isaac Touro watched over the Synagogue during the American Revolution when most of the Jewish population fled Newport,and the building was being used as a hospital for the British military.

Houses of worship aren't the only firsts in Rhode Island. In June of 1772, the first movement against British soldiers took place in Warwick at Namquid Point (now known as Gaspee Point).The Gaspee Incident, as it is historically known, was the burning of the British schooner, Gaspee. This event has been called the "first blow

149

for freedom," as it took place about a year and a half before the more historically famous Boston Tea Party incident.

The sailors from the Gaspee, and many other pirate ships, most likely stopped and drank rum at the White Horse Tavern while traveling through Newport. This is the nation's first and oldest Tavern. Originally built as a two-story residential home in 1652, the residence was converted toThe White Horse Tavern in 1673 and has become a 'bucket list' bar for modern day tourists from around the globe who enjoy visiting historic watering holes.

Rhode Islanders can certainly boast that the first and longest running Fourth of July parade started in Bristol back in 1785. Reverend Henry Wright of the First Congregational Church was a Revolutionary War veteran and is credited for being the local native who began this Independence Day celebration.

Slater Mill in Pawtucket is known as the "Birthplace of the Industrial Revolution." Samuel Slater started the first operating industrial Mill in the United States. Powered by a water wheel, Slater Mill was built in 1793 to manufacture thread out of cotton. This was its soul production until 1829 when various owners and renters occupied the building over the course of many years and manufactured other goods such as cardboard, coffin trimmings, and tools for the jewelry industry.

In addition to revolutionizing manufacturing, Pawtucket also has the Modern Diner, which is the first diner in the country to be included on the National Register of Historic Places.

Although it has recently undergone a restoration that includes 48 micro-loft residences, the Arcade in Providence is the nation's first and oldest indoor shopping mall. When it first opened back in 1828, the building comprised entirely of retail stores. Now, the ground floor still houses specialty, boutique-style retail shops, and the second and third floors are home to micro-loft apartments, giving this historic landmark a unique blend of residential and retail spaces, which has created a thriving community in downtown Providence's financial district.

For a city of just under 200,000 residents, Providence has a plethora of theater companies that is well-supported by Rhode Islanders statewide giving the capital city a thriving theater scene. One theater of historic significance is The Players at Barker Playhouse, which was founded in 1909 and is the oldest continuously running little theater in America.

Also in Providence on the corner of Charles and Corliss Streets is the first automated post office in the world. It was dedicated on October 20, 1960, and incorporated the first high-speed sorting, facing, and canceling machines. These machines have helped make mail processing faster, more efficient, and better able to handle the growing volume of mail the antiquated machines during that time had difficulty keeping up with the demand.

Having over 400 miles of shoreline, Rhode Island is well known for its beaches. In the southwestern-most corner of the state, Watch Hill not only has a beautiful beach and a mansion owned by Taylor Swift, but it is also known for having the oldest continuously operating carousel in the United States. The Flying Horse Carousel was brought to Watch Hill in 1883 and is unique in that the horses are suspended by chains, making it the only flying horse carousel in the country, and only kids who are under five feet tall and weigh less than 100 pounds are allowed to ride it.

In a state that is only 48 miles long and 37 miles wide, there are quite a few unique gems for just under one million residents and its visitors to enjoy in such a small area, many of which Rhode Islanders can be take pride in doing first.

Hello Rhode Island

by Jimmy Gyasi Boateng

One of the best tourist attractions in Rhode Island is Water Fire. It's a state-of-the-art attraction that brightens the city. People travel from all over the world to see this magnificent work.

Though Rhode Island has the Tennis Hall of Fame located in Newport, nothing compares to Water Fire when it comes to tourism. Newport also has glamourous mansions, yacht clubs, and tall ships, yet Water Fire still ranks as one of the best attractions. The water display that includes ancient canoes that go back and forth is fantastic.

Rhode Island is in my heart. Sweet Little Rhody. The state is officially named and registered as The State of Rhode Island and Providence Plantations. People from the outside call her capitol city Providence. "Providence" is a biblical word that means God has blessed the city.

The state is surrounded by the ocean. Water, water, water everywhere. Seafood is available in every restaurant. If one is allergic to seafood, one should take two steps back.

We do not just lie on our beautiful beaches; the ocean gives us the tallest and richest seafood varieties, which includes lobsters, shrimp, crab and salmon just to name a few.

Also, Rhode Island is bordered by two big states – Massachusetts and Connecticut. However, believe me, they will never absorb us in any way because the state is too independent all on its own. After all, what else do we need? We have Brown University, one of the most renowned universities in the country. Our contribution to the world is huge. We we train top doctors, engineers, architects, writers and well-known politicians.

In a very short time, Rhode Island is going to improve and expand its airport to become a first-class international destination. That will be very nice because it will bring more people here to improve our tourism and boost our economy.

Kudos to our governor, Gina Raimondo, for her effortful work. More grease to her elbow.

One important place that every tourist who comes here should visit is Federal Hill which boasts exquisite restaurants, pizza places, and clubs.

We are the state which can boast to have started the textile revolution, as Slater Mill in Pawtucket proves.

The jewelry industry is slowing in Rhode Island. We used to be the world's leader in the industry. Our airport is decorated with jewelry. Women who wear our jewelry look as sharp and beautiful as queens.

Hospitality in Rhode Island is second to none. Johnson and Wales University has special programs where students study to become experts in the culinary field.

Smiling faces and friendly people are what keeps the torch burning. Rhode Island will always be in my heart.

Hey, folks out there, don't leave home without your luck. Maybe your visit to Rhode Island will be your fifteen minutes of fame when you win big at the slot machines at the Twin River Casino.

Can you dance and do you also love food and fun? Then here is the place for you – The Newport Jazz Festival. It is an annual affair where people travel from across the continent to come here and have fun. There is music, food, fun, and dance. This is a stress-free festival where people dance from noon to dawn. Woodstock was a once in a lifetime historical event. The Newport Jazz Festival is an annual affair.

Wow! Talking about the Olympic Games and the prestigious award of G-O-L-D medals. The Ocean State already has a gold medal under her belt. The state is a leader in yacht racing and was the host of the America's Cup. What great achievements. Congratulations, Rhode Island.

And there is the Bristol Fourth of July Parade. It is the oldest in the country. We celebrate our independence in a special way. Broadway and Hollywood do not have it, but the Ocean State does. Who does not like the fanfare of the marching bands, the floats and the crowd?

Good luck and keep a smile on your face.

Don't say I'm a coward. Honestly, some things make my stomach growl, and some things give me goosebumps. Rhode Island has ghost hunters and many haunted houses.

Assuming you enter into one of these houses during Halloween and from nowhere a wild ghost jumps on you and screams – YUCK! Which direction are you gonna run? Please don't call me to come to your rescue – call the cops.

Oh! Lord have mercy on me. Amen.

Then there is Roger Williams Park, the museum, the zoo and the wild animals. Rhode Islanders are lucky to have all these exuberant recreational centers. Africa is here with us and wild animal lovers do not have to travel far. Come on down and visit – we open our arms wide to you.

Mother Nature is wonderful for Rhode Islanders. There is good landscaping and beautifully green golf courses. I am a bit old and can't swing golf clubs well as it hurts my back. My shoulders are also not strong enough for me to be a caddy. That does not mean I do not enjoy the game. I love it. I enjoy the young players and watch the game from the sidelines. Golf clubhouses have delicious cuisine, entrees, appetizers, and beer that make my mouth water. Life is fun. I will always enjoy my life.

In conclusion, I would not be surprised if one day, Rhode Island bids for the Olympics and wins the chance to bring the games here.

Come and discover the beauty of Rhode Island and its hospitable people.

A Life Was Saved

by Victor C. Rudowski

I'm guessing that some of the men and women of our beloved organization, the Association of Rhode Island Authors, who, besides writing, may also enjoy fishing. I'm also confident that many of our authors may have begun their fishing experience in fresh water. Yes we are residents of the "Ocean State", but it's obvious that a large proportion of people living in Rhode Island are not very close to the ocean and probably first learned to fish in some of our fresh water ponds, lakes and rivers.

I grew up in Olneyville section of Providence and began fishing when I was about eight years old. At that age we always had a grownup with us to keep us safe and to teach us how to fish. When I was eleven or twelve years old me and many friends in the neighborhood completed swimming lessons at the Olneyville Boys Club, and so after becoming teenagers we were allowed to go fishing as a group, but never alone. All of the kids in my neighborhood fished in the Woonasquatucket River near Merino Park in Olneyville. Believe it or not we caught a lot of fish in that river - mostly Carp and Sunfish. Back in the early 1950's I'm not sure if anyone was remotely aware of the pollution that existed in the river. I'm also guessing that pollution wasn't much of a social or political issue at that time. Not surprisingly, most of the pollution was caused by the discharge of chemicals and other wastes from many of the textile and manufacturing plants that operated alongside the river. Maybe the mind-set in those days was that if the fish and other animals could live in that water then how bad could the water really be. Fortunately, even though we swam in the river, I know that we never ate any of the fish that we caught. The term "catch and release" was not an obvious fishing slogan or a prescribed practice in those days, but it was exactly what we always did. As for swimming in the river, I'm sure that we probably swallowed some river water on occasion and fortunately I'm still here to talk about it.

My friend John and I began trout fishing when we hit our teen years, and if I recall correctly, the fishing license for our age group in those days cost about fifty-cents. There was no "Trout Stamp" required in those days either. How times have changed. Today, a fresh water fishing license costs eighteen dollars for a resident. Back then you fished in the ocean for free, while today you need a license for ocean fishing and the cost is seven dollars for a resident. The license is free for residents over the age of 65. Whoopee!

In Rhode Island, the fresh water fishing season always begins at sun-up, on the second Saturday in April. Back in the 1950's you could begin fishing when the clock struck midnight on that special Saturday in April. At that time we were too young to drive so we usually got a ride from either one of our parents or an older friend who had a drivers license. The usual routine was that we would be dropped off around 10:30 or 11:00 PM and then picked up the next day around 10:00 AM. We always packed a bag of "goodies" to munch on during the night. Before our parents dropped us off they always warned us to be safe and to stay out of "trouble". "Come on mom and dad, what kind of trouble can we get into whenever we go fishing?" Well, we would soon find out!

We always went to our favorite trout fishing hole — Peck Pond in Casimir Pulaski State Park. This very popular park is located off of Route 44 in the town of Chepachet, right near the Connecticut state line. If you are facing North, Peck Pond is shaped like an inverted letter "Y". The south-western end of the pond is located in Connecticut and licensed fishermen from either state are allowed to fish the entire pond.

As best as I can recollect, John and I were either 14 or 15 years old when the terrible incident occurred. That would have made it either 1958 or 1959. Recalling those days, I can remember one opening "night" at Pulaski when the temperature was so cold that ice had formed in the eyelets of our fishing rods. Fortunately on this particular evening we had pleasant spring weather which made it a little easier to get through the night. Nonetheless, the water was still very cold.

I always remember silently cursing the older adults who had fly rods and full waders who fished waist deep in the water off the park beach and caught all the trout, or so we believed. They even had "creels" attached to their waders to hold and hide their catch. Kids like us just had spinning rods and we either used a worm and float or cast and retrieved a gold or silver spinner lure. Occasionally we might catch a trout, but most of the time we got "skunked". We didn't really care because the fun of it was being out all night without any grownups supervising us. There were always hundreds of people fishing on opening "night" so you can imagine that our night along the shoreline was not very quiet. Everyone seemed to be using either flashlights or camping lanterns to see what they were doing. John and I could only afford to bring "stick" matches to use as needed. We surely could have used one of those tiny LED flash lights that are so popular today.

Long before dawn, John and I had moved around the pond quite a bit, searching for the perfect spot along the shoreline to catch our "limit". Sometimes kids can be very optimistic. Of course we never found that perfect spot but we sure as heck tried. When dawn finally broke we decided to move around to the eastern side of the pond where we knew there would be fewer people fishing. Our misguided philosophy then was "the fewer the fishermen, the more the fish". The path around that side of the pond was not easy to navigate, even if you had a flash light, so waiting for the sun to rise was the smart thing for us to do.

Along most of the shore line on the Eastern side of the pond there are lateral paths leading from the main path to the water. These lateral paths can easily hold one or two fishermen. As we walked the pond, all of the lateral paths were already occupied by other fishermen, so we continued on towards the end of the pond, hoping to find one empty spot. As we approached each "occupied" path we always made a comment of "any luck" to the fishermen who we encountered. Of course the usual response was always "nah, no luck". Yeah sure! I guess most fishermen usually have this same response. Deny! Deny! Deny! Maybe it's part of our fishing DNA. Do you want some good advice? Never believe what a fisherman tells you. Of course I say this in total jest.

When we arrived at the northern east-end of the pond there were only two lateral paths left and the closest one was occupied by a "fly-rod guy". He was up to his waist in the water, flipping his line back and forth. We said hello with our usual how's-your-luck comment and got the usual response. We moved on to the last path and were happy to see that it was empty and waiting for us. When fishing on the northern end of the pond, each lateral path to the water was hidden from view to other adjacent paths due to bushes, trees and all kinds of shore growth. This meant that you most likely could not see your neighbor, let alone know if they were having any "luck". After about twenty "luckless" minutes we heard a splash to our left and John and I looked at each other in total confusion. From the sound, we knew that this wasn't a fish fighting for its life. John and I laid our rods on the ground and hurried over to the path where we knew the splash sound had come from. We were both shocked at what we discovered. The fisherman was lying face down in the water with his arms stretched out in front of him. Even worse, he wasn't moving. We looked at each other again and immediately knew what we had to do. That damn water was really cold when we waded in to help the man. When we reached him we were able to flip him over on his back and drag him back onto the shore. He was a very heavy dude. Of course a lot of the weight was from water that had accumulated inside his waders. When we pulled him on shore the poor man began foaming at the mouth, and he then began to cough and spit up water even though he seemed to be unconscious. At this point we were a little confused as to what we should do. The term 'CPR' and the practice of "Cardio-Pulmonary-Resuscitation" as we know it today was not in vogue at that time, and our obvious lack of medical training prevented us from directly helping the man. I could always run faster than John so I volunteered to go get help. As I began running back to the beach I noticed that the two spots to the left of where we had rescued the fisherman were now unoccupied. That's probably why no other fishermen had heard the "splash".

It didn't take me long to get back to the beach area and find a park ranger. I explained the problem and the ranger immediately radioed for medical help. In the interim I explained where the man was located and volunteered to lead some adults back to help the man. I suggested that maybe a bunch of us could help carry the man back to the beach area. The park ranger agreed and directed me and four or five adults to head back to help the man and start moving him back towards the beach. The ranger himself had to wait until medical help arrived so that he could lead them to meet up with us along the path. When we got back to the spot where the man was lying, there were two adults helping to revive the man. The adults who followed me back immediately jumped in to assist. John and I were obviously relieved to have this burden lifted from our teenage shoulders. Medical personnel arrived pretty quickly and John and I went back to our fishing spot to retrieve our gear. It's amazing how wading waist deep into cold water will dampen one's desire to continue fishing.

John's dad was waiting for us when we got back to the beach area and we happily got in his car after explaining why we were so wet. His dad was astonished to hear our story and asked if we wanted to stay a little longer to see if the man had been revived. We chose to leave because we were cold and we knew there was nothing else we could possibly do for the man. Surprisingly, no one ever asked us who we were or if we knew the man whom we had pulled out of the water. To this day I wonder if he ever knew what we had done for him. At the time we thought that the man may have had an epileptic seizure or some such malady. John and I checked the Providence Journal Obituary Section every day for a few days to see if some man had died while fishing. Nothing was ever reported. The only thing I recall about the man was that he was heavy-set, had dark hair and that we had a very difficult time dragging him out of the water. I also remember that he was wearing a gold ring with a ruby colored stone; it might have been either a college ring or a high-school ring. I'm also guessing that his fly-rod is still lying at the bottom of Peck Pond. Who knows? I hope that the poor man survived the episode and lived a long and healthy life, filled with great fishing memories. When I think about the incident I always wonder if the man knew that two young teenagers saved his life that morning. I hope he did. If we had decided to stay at our previous fishing spot, would there have been a sad headline in Sunday's Providence Journal?

I haven't seen my old friend John since we graduated from high school and I often wonder how he is doing. I joined the Air Force right after graduation and while I was away in the service, my parents moved from Providence to Johnston. Because of the move, I lost track of most of my previous neighborhood friends. On a few occasions I drove around the old neighborhood to look for some of my old friends, but just like me, they too had moved away. I guess each of us went on to live our lives as best we could. Times change and so do we. I'm so happy that John and I went fishing that night, even though we didn't catch any trout. One might say that we caught a "life" instead.

About the Authors

Al Bettencourt is the Author of Nicky's Story, a real-life story of an incredible dog who seemed to have multiple lives. Al has spent most of his life devoted to agriculture in RI. He grew up on a farm in Warren, RI where he and his father farmed 17 acres of sweet corn and native vegetables. He was appointed as the State Executive Director of the Agricultural Stabilization and Conservation Service in 1981. In 2000, he was appointed the Executive Director of the RI Farm Bureau, the largest farm organization in RI. Among his duties was writing the agency's newsletter and producing a monthly TV show on cable. He retired from that position in 2015. He and his wife Gail run a small farm in Burrillville and have an honor stand. Al is the president of the Burrillville Farmer's Market.

Jimmy Gyasi Boateng, a native of Ghana, served in that country's parliament for ten years before going to work as a librarian at the State Insurance Corporation of Ghana. He moved to the United States in 1978 and has worked for numerous employers, including serving as an interpreter for the Massachusetts judiciary. He graduated from Rhode Island Trade Shops School earning a diploma in culinary arts as well as a certificate from the New England Gerontology Academy. He has been voted three times to the board of trustees for the American Amalgamated Clothing and Textile Workers Union Local-1832T.

Helen Burke has been writing and performing poetry for 45 years. Her new collection, *Today the Birds Will Sing* is out with Valley Press. See www.krazyphils.co.uk for other books and artwork. She is also a visual artist and radio show host. She holds a master's degree in literature.

Paul F. Caranci is a historian and the award-winning author of eight books. The former RI Deputy Secretary of State also served on his local Town Council for over sixteen years. His experiences working undercover with the FBI for seventeen months to gather video and audio taped evidence of a widespread corruption scheme is the subject of *Wired: A Shocking True Story of Political Corruption and the FBI Informant Who*

Risked Everything to Expose it (2017) Two of Paul's books, *The Hanging & Redemption of John Gordon* (2012) and *Scoundrels* (2016) were each named non-fiction book of the year. Visit Paul's website at www.paulcaranci.com.

R.N. Chevalier published his first novel, *Are We the Klingons*, in 2015, three years after he was diagnosed with ALS. His second novel, *Advances of the Ancients*, was released in 2016 and *Full Circle* in 2017. They comprise a science-fiction action adventure trilogy with erotic undertones.

He co-authored a book with his wife, Donna, titled *Rhode Island Civil War Monuments—A Pictorial Guide*, which was also released in 2017. It is an artistic view of the state's monuments with their histories in the narrative. With each new book R.N. Chevalier demonstrates that no disability can keep the human spirit down.

Kathy Clark is a retired Firefighter/EMT-C turned author since 2009. She has written articles and stories about dogs, in particular, the St. Bernard breed that she and her husband have owned for the past 18 years. Her stories have appeared in *The New England St. Bernard Club Sentinel*, the *Pawtucket Times*, and *Shoreline* (Association of Rhode Island Authors Anthology, 2016).

Jane F. Collen tries to use her storytelling talent for good instead of evil. The award winning Enjella® Adventure Series was written as part of her crusade to encourage love for reading in children. Combining her experience as a lawyer, a part time teacher, a mother, an avid reader and lover of all genres of good books, Collen loves to invent stories.

In this coming year, Collen will publish another children's book and an historic romance.

While Collen is an Intellectual Property lawyer in New York she spends as much time in Westerly, RI as possible. Read her latest writings at www.enjella.com.

Jessica M. Collette has lived in three of the six New England states. The beauty and ever-changing seasons in this region have always inspired her. In addition to nature, she also writes about love, loss and striving to see life through a positive perspective. Her books, Your Special Star and Naming the Bits Between are dedicated to her son. Both books were written to provide encouragement and hope for those who have loved and lost someone close to them. Jessica lives in Rhode Island with her husband and an adorable Boston terrier. Visit www.jessicamcollette.com to view current musings and poetry.

Norman Desmarais, professor emeritus at Providence College, lives in Lincoln, RI. He is an active re-enactor, a member of *Le Regiment Bourbonnais*, the 2nd Rhode Island Regiment and the Brigade of the American Revolution. He is the author of *Battlegrounds of Freedom, The Guide to the American Revolutionary War* (6 volumes), and *The Guide to the American Revolutionary War at Sea and Overseas* (7 volumes). He has also translated the *Gazette Françoise*, the French newspaper published in Newport by the French fleet that brought the Count de Rochambeau and French troops to America in July 1780.

Leo C. Frisk, Jr. was born in Woonsocket, Rhode Island in 1950. When he was seven years-old, his family moved to a small country town in Massachusetts. It was here, living in a house with a backyard filled with woods and ponds, he grew up learning about and playing with all kinds of animals and insects. Catching snakes and turtles during the day and lightning bugs at night were just a few of his regular childhood adventures. But then as all boys do, he grew up, was soon married, and was blessed with a boy of his own. When his son was just two, Leo learned he was going blind. Unable to read any longer, he began to make up stories while pretending to read to his son. He soon discovered that his son liked his stories better than the ones that were actually in the books he was holding. Today, Leo is totally blind and writes his stories from the many childhood memories he has stored in his imagination. Because of this, he considers himself to be a 64 year-old boy with his wife Gail. Leo now resides in Harrisville, Rhode Island, in a small house in a rural area surrounded by neighbors who he considers friends. He spends his days caning chairs, working in his yard and writing children's stories using his talking computer—stories he hopes children of all ages will enjoy. He has written six books.

L.A. Jacob's family is from The Valley, a neighborhood of Cumberland located approximately from Cumberland Town Hall to St. Patrick's Catholic Church on Broad Street. Portuguese immigrants from the Azores in the 1920's, L.A.'s mother's uncle told her the family stories that got her interested in storytelling from a very early age. She lives in Central Falls, not too far from where her mother's family grew up. She normally writes magical fiction at www.grimaulkin.com, but returned to her Uncle Manny for the story in this anthology.

Debbie Kaiman Tillinghast is the author of *The Ferry Home*, a memoir about her childhood on Prudence Island, a tiny island off the coast of Rhode Island. Debbie began writing as she embarked on a quest to re-connect with her island roots, starting with a cookbook for her family.

She has been published in *Country Extra* magazine, and *Shoreline*, the first anthology published by the Association of Rhode Island Authors.

Debbie is a retired teacher and Nutrition Educator, and she now enjoys volunteering as well as writing, gardening, biking and spending time with her children and grandchildren.

Deborah Katz, a Rhode Islander, with a Boston University B.S. and two Master's from URI in Education and Counseling, has always enjoyed writing, especially poetry, since a child.

Deborah wrote and illustrated a book about a dolphin, which became a favorite with her classes the last 24 years of her teaching. She plans to self-publish the book, wishing to for it to continue to bring many children hope and a smile.

Deborah has extensively researched health and nutrition, since the 1970's. By self-publishing a special cookbook, utilizing some of that information, she hopes to benefit the health and outlook of others.

Lawrence J. Krips is an evolution coach, gatherings leader and poet. A founding member of Ocean State Poets and contributor to the Origami Poetry Project, Larry's poetry has appeared in *Tifferet, Rhode Island Writers' Circle Anthology, New Verse News, The Best of Kindness II anthology, Love's Chance Magazine, The Open Door* and *50 Haikus*. He has appeared with the musical group, *Mouthpeace* and *Thunder and The Bird*. In 2012 Mr. Krips received a Pushcart Prize nomination for his poem **Yahrzeit**. His first book, *A Soul's Way... Soulspeak* was published last year by Hallowed Abyss. Larry may be contacted at illuminationcoaching@aol.com

Susan Letendre lives in a tiny house, on a tiny lake, in the tiniest state of Rhode Island. She is a grateful environmental educator, storyteller, and peace and justice activist. Her activism led her to travel to Cuba, where she met Saulo Serrano, with whom she shares a similar life philosophy. It is he whose illustrations bring this story of to life. Susan believes in, and writes and tells about, the connectedness of all things.

Frances L. O'Donnell received one of the first annual "Dorry Awards" for her Poetry book, *Whispers from The Tree of Life*, honoring the very best in local literature, book of the year award on September 27, 2016. *Whispers from The Tree of Life* also received an Honorable Mention from The Paris Book Festival Competition on May 17, 2016. In *Whispers from the Tree of Life*, Fran O'Donnell's poetry sparkles with the deeply hued jewels of her mind and heart. Her poetry reflects myriad colors and feelings combined with keen observations. Fran's poetry beguiles in its playful simplicity and surprises with its transcendent meaning. Fran celebrates the beauty of the natural world and a hunger to connect with it. The poet invites us not to be afraid of life but to embrace it tenderly with love and gratitude. Most importantly, she encourages us to discover our own bright star. Eileen M. Stefani MA. English --- Phi Beta Kappa Connecticut College Artist ---Natural Science Illustration Society.

Christie O'Neil Harrison has been writing poetry since she was 9 years old. Much of her work tends to focus on nature, the senses, and spirituality. Her first book, *Dear Tommy*, was published in 2008. It is a grief journal that she wrote as a tribute to her younger brother who had died tragically in 1994. Her second book, *Collecting Seashells by the Seashore*, is a collection of her poetry and essays, published in 2014. Christie lives in Pawtucket with her children and enjoys walking and singing.

Joanne Perella is a Southie who moved to Rhode Island when she was four. She has always been an avid writer. Most recently she was an essayist on NPR.

Mark Perry is a former journalist who turned children's author back in 2010 when he founded www.northpolepostman.com. This BBB accredited website is the cornerstone to his created character, 'Post' Mark, the elf who works in Santa's mailroom. He wrote, *Rhode Island, A State of*

Firsts for this anthology from the research he gathered for his latest children's book, *'Post' Mark – The North Pole Postman Visits Rhode Island*, the follow up to his debut title, *'Post' Mark – Santa's Misfit Postman*. Perry grew up in North Attleboro, Massachusetts, but currently resides in the Elmhurst neighborhood of Providence, Rhode Island's "Creative Capital."

Joni Pfeiffer-Moser's love of writing began in high school as co-feature editor of the school newspaper. College years highlighted English, journalism and children's literature. Her career in radio and television required much creative writing. Featured in two Anthologies of Wakefield's Neighborhood Writing Guild, she's had articles in the *Providence Journal* and *Independent*. In 2016 and 2017, her poetry was featured in the Wickford Art Association's Poetry & Art Exhibit. Joni's first children's book, *Annie, the Story of an Apple*, was published last year. She lives in Wakefield juggling her writing life with family, friends, a book club, theater, and concerts.

Dawn M. Porter, author of *Searching for Rhode Island*, is a special education and history teacher from the quintessential Rhode Island mill village of Harmony, where she lives with her husband and two children. She is a publisher and bookstore owner.

Steven R. Porter is the author of two novels: the critically-acclaimed Southie crime-thriller *Confessions of the Meek & the Valiant*, and the award-winning historical novel *Manisses* inspired by the rich history of Block Island. He is also the co-author of *Scared to Death... Do It Anyway* a self-help guide for individuals who suffer from anxiety and panic attacks. Steven speaks frequently to schools and libraries about his books, trends in independent publishing, and on special topics in writing and marketing. He and his wife Dawn own Stillwater River Publications, Stillwater Books, and he is founder and president of the Association of Rhode Island Authors.

Lénore M. Rhéaume, a RI native, writes in English and Canadian French. She studied Liberal Arts at Barrington College, RI. She received an A.S. degree and a B.A. in English from the UMF, Maine. Her work appeared in *Coastlines*, the *Kennebec Journal* and in *They Work, We Write* anthology.

She is a member of Ocean State Poets and ARIA. In 2015, she edited, published a reference series of ecumenical articles for a RI clergyman. She produces a RI TV show, "Poets and Poems," TV specials. and publications for other authors. Her French poems are featured on WNRI, Woonsocket.

Victor C. Rudowski is a retired computer programmer living in West Warwick. He acquired his love for fiction during a four-year term in the U.S. Air Force in the early 60's. He has written articles for the Rhode Island Saltwater Anglers Association (RISSA) of which he is a longtime member. After graduating from programming school, he began his programming career in banking and enrolled in evening classes at Providence College where he earned a B.A. in English. He is currently completing his first novel and hopes to have it published within the next year.

Edward Taylor has been writing ever since his parents bought him a journal and he decided to try his hand at fiction instead. A lifelong Rhode Island native, he attended East Providence High School and graduated from Rhode Island College in 2013. Working in government to keep the student bill collectors at bay, he spends much of his free time streaming television and apologizing to his roommate while he learns the violin. The author of two unpublished fiction manuscripts, he is currently seeking an agent while building additional writing credits. He can be reached at etaylor0802@gmail.com or on Twitter @Edward_Taylor90.

Tom Trabulsi was born in the Midwest, attended high school in Rhode Island, and graduated from Boston University. After college, he became a bike courier in Boston and New York City. Later, these adventures would be chronicled in his first novel, *Sandaman's Riposte*. After moving to Colorado, he worked construction throughout the Rocky Mountains. *Forked Head Pass*, his current novel about the Colorado land rush in the late 1990s, is in its final edit. Currently, he is a firefighter in Pawtucket, Rhode Island. *Code Red*, his next project, is already in the works.

Barbara Ann Whitman still remembers her very first writing assignment: a poem about Peggy, her family's Boston Terrier, that she wrote when she was in the first grade. Since then, she has produced poetry, essays, editorials, news stories, blogs and song lyrics. She recently completed her first young adult novel reflecting her 25 years of experience as a Child Abuse Investigator. Her other interests include photography, antiques, camping, dancing, and the beach. She sings in her church choir and is a member of the Old Fiddlers Club of Rhode Island. She was the original organizer of a meet-up group for active seniors called The Quick Silvers. Currently, she lives in Johnston and is a '30 Days to Family' Specialist at Foster Forward.

Bruce Wilcox, from North Smithfield, R.I. is a Mechanical Engineer by day, and a children's author by evening.

From his time serving with the Boy Scouts of America, Troop 1139 Slatersville, RI, he has enjoyed teaching life skills to young minds.

The author has a love of history and a passion for Genealogy. He has been researching military history and his family descendants since 1992.

For the past six years he has been creating a children's story called *Sheep Tales, the Story of Clara & Tobey.* The book is scheduled to be released in the Fall 2017.

ISBN-10: 0-692-73383-3
ISBN-13: 978-069273-383-7
$10.00

ISBN-10: 1-976-07999-3
ISBN-13: 978-197607-999-3
$10.00

Available at online retailers, bookstores and
www.StillwaterPress.com

ORDER FORM

Please use the following to order additional copies of

Under the 13th Star (2017) and/or *Shoreline* (2016)
Selected Short Fiction, Nonfiction, Poetry and Prose from The Association of Rhode Island Authors

_____ (QTY) **Under the 13th Star**   X $10.00 Total $_____

_____ (QTY)   **Shoreline**   X $10.00 Total $_____

**Shipping & Handling $_____

GRAND TOTAL $_____

**Shipping & Handling: Please add $3.00 for the first copy, and $1.50 for each additional copy.

Payment Method:

___ Personal Check Enclosed (Payable to ARIA)

___ Charge my Credit Card

Name:_____ BILLING ZIP CODE:_____

Visa____MC_____Amex_____ Discover____

Card Number:_____ EXP:_____/_____CSC_____

Signature:_____

Ship To:

Name _____

Street _____

City _____State:_____Zip:_____

Phone _____Email:_____

___Check to add to ARIA's email list.

MAIL YOUR COMPLETED FORM TO:
The Association of Rhode Island Authors (ARIA)
c/o Stillwater River Publications
63 Sawmill Road
Chepachet, RI 02814
info@stillwaterpress.com
www.StillwaterPress.com
www.RIAuthors.org

Made in the USA
Columbia, SC
13 October 2017